BOOK SEVEN

D1596371

BARNABAS COLLINS SEARCHES FOR A WAY TO END THE CENTURIES-OLD CURSE OF A JEALOUS WOMAN.

You'll thrill to this spine-tingling adventures of your favorite vampire as Barnabas Collins searches for the woman who will replace his long-lost Josette and end the terrible curse of Angelique.

This never-before-told story of the handsome, mysterious vampires who has captured the hearts of the millions of viewers of ABC-TV's suspense drama, DARK SHADOWS, will delight every one of his fans.

Hermes Press

Published by Hermes Press, an imprint of
Herman and Geer Communications, Inc.

Daniel Herman, Publisher
Troy Musguire, Production Manager
Eileen Sabrina Herman, Managing Editor
Alissa Fisher, Graphic Design
Kandice Hartner, Senior Editor

2100 Wilmington Road
Neshannock, Pennsylvania 16105
(724) 652-0511
www.HermesPress.com; info@hermespress.com

Book design by Eileen Sabrina Herman
First printing, 2020

LCCN applied for: 10 9 8 7 6 5 4 3 2 1 0
ISBN 978-1-61345-212-7
OCR and text editing by H + G Media and Eileen Sabrina Herman
Proof reading by Eileen Sabrina Herman and Theresa Halvorsen

From Dan, Louise, Sabrina, Jacob, Ruk'us and Noodle for D'zur and Mellow

Acknowledgments: This book would not be possible without the help and encouragement of Jim Pierson and Curtis Holdings

Printed in Canada

THE SECRET OF
BARNABAS COLLINS
by Marilyn Ross

CONTENTS

CONTENTS

CHAPTER 1

From the moment on a bleak April night when Victoria Winters had opened the front door of Collinwood to find herself confronted with a tall, handsome stranger in a caped coat, she had been under the spell of Barnabas Collins' charm. He had stood there briefly silhouetted against the cloudy sky and then he'd bowed in a courtly manner.

"I have come to see my cousin Elizabeth Stoddard," he said in a deep rich voice with a pleasant English accent. "I trust she is at home."

"Please come in," Victoria had invited him. "Who shall I tell Mrs. Stoddard is calling?"

Leaning a little on the silver-headed black cane he carried, he told her with a smile, "Say it is her cousin, Barnabas Collins, from England. I'm sure she's familiar with our branch of the family. My father and grandfather have been here before me."

Victoria tried not to stare. But he was such an unusual, magnetic type she could not help herself. His melancholy face with its high cheekbones and deep-set eyes was almost cadaverous; yet he was a romantic figure. The thick black hair in casual disarray across his intelligent forehead added to his dash. And when he spoke his somewhat heavy lips revealed glistening white teeth.

She said, "I'll tell Mrs. Stoddard you're here. Please take a chair in the living room." And she hurried upstairs to tell the older woman about her visitor.

That was how Barnabas Collins had arrived at Collinwood in 1968. In a few days he was installed in the old house at the rear of the grounds—a house for which he seemed to have a strange sentimental attachment. Nothing was seen of him during the daylight hours. But in the evenings he often wandered about the grounds. The old family cemetery held great interest for him. He spent hours jotting down inscriptions from gravestones. He explained to Victoria that he was authoring a history of the Collins family and he was gaining information of great importance.

He also seemed to enjoy wandering along the cliffs and staring out at the breakers as they lashed against the rocky shore. His solitary figure was a familiar sight there at dusk, and he often strolled to the ruins of the ancient stone house, once known as Stormcliff, which had burned down almost a century before.

One evening in June as the twilight gradually was fading to darkness Victoria came upon him by the weed-and brush-filled yawning cellar, which with a few remaining stones of the original walls fringing it, was all that remained of the once noble Stormcliff. She also had been taking a stroll in the pleasant evening on her own.

He turned to greet her, smiling. "Are you too interested in the ruins of Stormcliff?"

She shrugged. "In a way. There is a print of it hanging in the library at Collinwood. It must be very old. And it shows the house as a beautiful old place."

"It was," the tall, handsome Englishman said, staring at the gaping cellar again. And then he gave her a quick glance with those hypnotic, deep-set eyes and quietly added, "What I mean is, I'm sure it must have been. Such a magnificent location, and the cellar indicates how large it was. Tragic that it should have been ravaged by fire."

"I've always felt so," she agreed. "Roger Collins claims a lot of the stones that didn't topple into the cellar were stolen over the years by people in the area who wanted to use them for building. Of course he feels this was very wrong since Stormcliff was part of the Collins property."

"I can sympathize with Cousin Roger in this," Barnabas said with a sigh. He pointed his silver-headed cane in the direction of the dark mass of Collinwood and added, "It's not more than five minutes to the main house."

"I know little about Stormcliff or who lived in it," Victoria said. "But then, I haven't been here long."

Barnabas regarded her with interest. "So I understand. Shall we take the path along the cliffs on the way back? It's longer but interesting just as night falls. And we have each other for company."

"I'd like that," Victoria said. She had worn a light sweater over her sleeveless dress, since even summer nights in Maine generally held a certain chill. Tossing back her shoulder length black hair, she began to slowly stroll with the impressive stranger to the edge of the cliffs.

It was so close to darkness that she could barely make out his face. He swung the black walking stick with a certain grace as he kept in step with her. Then, far above them, a gull circled and uttered a melancholy cry that for reasons unknown to her suddenly sent a chill racing through her slim youthful body.

Barnabas must have sensed her feeling of sudden fear for he glanced at her as they continued along the path by the cliff's edge. "Night's black mantle covers all alike," he said with an unexpected gentleness as his hand touched her arm. "You must not fear it."

She forced a smile on her sensitive face. "I guess I might as well admit it. I share that fear with most people. A dread of the unknown. A terror of what the shadows may hold."

"You must try to conquer your fears," he went on in the same soft voice. "Night is a blessed time between day and day. It is only in these hours I feel truly alive."

The touch of his hand on her arm thrilled her. She glanced up at his shadowy figure. "You do enjoy the dark, don't you?" she said. "In fact, I never have seen you during the daylight hours."

He laughed lightly. "I claim the eccentricity due an author. I become so absorbed in the notes for my book I don't like to be disturbed from my desk during the day."

"But you shouldn't work too hard at it."

Far out at the end of a breakwater a lighthouse flashed a fingered light of warning across the darkness.

"And what about you?" he demanded. "Aren't you a kind of slave for Elizabeth and the family? I'd say you are the one who works too hard."

"Not really," she told him in a serious voice. "Elizabeth and the others have been good to me. And I like all the work I'm doing. I came here as a tutor for David but I became more a companion to Elizabeth."

"Elizabeth tells me you've had an unhappy love affair," Barnabas said as they walked on.

"Yes, Ernest Collins was killed just as we were about to make plans for our wedding," she said in a small voice. "I haven't really gotten over it yet."

"Tragic romance is not easy to bear," Barnabas said with understanding. "I have reason to know."

She looked up at the tall, shadowed figure. "But you must be very happy!" she protested. "I can't think of you having any romantic troubles."

"But then, you know so little about me," he reminded her.

"That is so," she admitted. "Though I tend to forget it. You've only been at Collinwood a short time, yet somehow it seems you belong here."

He nodded. "It's strange. I get that same feeling."

"And why shouldn't you?" she said. "Your ancestor, the original Barnabas Collins, left here for England about a hundred and seventy-five years ago. But according to what I've heard, members of your family have returned to visit the home place at intervals down through the years. Several of them were named after that first Barnabas Collins, just as you are."

"Returning has been like a homecoming."

"I'd expect you to be lonely. You should have a wife and perhaps children with you."

He halted suddenly. "I have always been a lonely man," he agreed. "I won't deny that. Nor will I argue that my heart is tied to the past."

Victoria smiled. "Your book! But you shouldn't allow it to devour you, to rule your whole life."

There was a brief moment of silence during which she could feel his eyes upon her. "If things were different and you were not such a child I would take that as encouragement."

She felt her cheeks burn. "Please!"

He raised a deprecating hand. "Of course I understood what you meant. And I'm very grateful to you for your concern. I'm not so sure I'm such a favorite with all the members of the Collins family."

"Yes!" she protested. "They are all fond of you. Carolyn, Elizabeth and even Roger. And Burke Devlin thinks you should buy yourself some property here and settle down. He says Collinsport could do with a proper English squire."

"Ah, Burke," Barnabas said with approval. "He is a fine man. And, I think, very fond of you. Why not allow your broken heart to mend and consider Burke seriously?"

She shook her head. "I'm not ready for that yet."

"Then there still may be hope for me." And with that he drew her close to touch his lips to her forehead.

Victoria's reaction was strange. Almost all the warm good feeling between them which she'd felt so strongly up until now fled from her. The embrace made her tremble. And the touch of his lips was so icy cold that she almost cried out her fear. The roar of the waves below suddenly assumed a startling loudness and further heightened the bleak sensation of being caught up in some terror of the night.

Barnabas gently released her. "You're trembling," he said. "I've frightened you. I'm sorry. It was an impulse."

"There's no need to apologize," she said half-heartedly. Embarrassed at her display of nerves, but still avoiding looking at him, she turned toward Collinwood which was almost directly opposite them at this point in their stroll along the cliffs. "I must be getting back," she said. "Elizabeth may worry about me."

"Of course," he said and again his hand sought her arm as he guided her across the lawn towards the old mansion. She was still shaken and uneasy but she tried to cover this by talking lightly.

The following morning she told Elizabeth of her meeting with Barnabas near the ruins of Stormcliff without mentioning any of the details of the walk and the weird feeling she'd experienced when he'd unexpectedly kissed her. She instead stressed his interest in the history of the burned house.

"The person he should meet and talk with is the vicar," Elizabeth said, interest showing on her maturely lovely face.

"Of course!" Victoria agreed. "I didn't think of that. But the vicar is a kind of specialist in local history."

Elizabeth smiled as they stood together in the garden. "Indeed he is. I'll arrange for you to take Barnabas over for a meeting with him."

And so on the evening of the following night she and the tall stranger from England made the rather long walk to the cottage of the vicar which was located on the road to Collinsport not far from the small Episcopal Church. Barnabas preferred walking to using a car.

It had rained during the day and now as night drew near there was still a light drizzle falling. She had put on a raincoat and kerchief but Barnabas in his familiar caped coat seemed not to mind the weather at all. He was hatless as usual and his black hair was plastered around his forehead from the wet. As they approached the vicar's cottage she saw the warm squares of yellow indicating his living room window.

She smiled up at Barnabas who had been walking in a kind of preoccupied silence. "The vicar must be waiting for us. I see he already has a light on in his living room."

He stared ahead with just a touch of uneasiness in his manner. "Perhaps we should not have troubled him."

"He'll be glad to see us," she reassured him. "He's a bachelor and rather lonely."

The stout old vicar greeted them cordially at the door and then had them sit with him in easy chairs facing the log fire in the tiny but spotlessly clean living room. At once he began to discuss the history of the town and the Collins family in particular. His bald dome reflected the flickering glow from the logs, and his chubby, florid face was full of interest as he stared at Barnabas seated opposite him.

"It's most remarkable," the old clergyman said.

"Indeed?" Barnabas inquired casually, his hands resting on the black cane with its silver wolf's head handle.

The vicar chuckled. "I neglected to explain my thoughts," he apologized. "But since you entered this room I've been struck by your resemblance to the first Barnabas Collins who lived almost two centuries ago. You must have seen his portrait in the hallway of Collinwood?"

Barnabas frowned. "Possibly. I can't recall having noticed it."

Victoria smiled. "No, Mrs. Stoddard has had the portrait removed while the wall is being repainted. So Mr. Collins hasn't seen it."

"What a pity!" the stout old parson said. And then he sat forward in his chair as if a sudden idea had come to him. "One moment! I've photographed nearly all the portraits at Collinwood for my collection. I'm sure I have one of the first Barnabas Collins. I'll take a look." And he rose slowly from his chair.

Barnabas raised a restraining hand. "Please don't bother!"

"No bother," the vicar assured him heartily as he went off to rummage in a cabinet at the other end of the room.

There was a short silence during which Barnabas gave her a look of grim resignation. She could tell that he was far from enjoying himself even though he and the clergyman shared a mutual interest. And when the old man returned triumphantly with a colored snapshot in one hand and an ancient ivory hand mirror in the other Victoria guessed that the visitor from England would have liked to flee from the room.

The vicar thrust both the snapshot and mirror into Barnabas' hands. "Look at that snapshot and then at yourself in the mirror. I tell you the likeness is amazing!"

Barnabas politely eyed the snapshot, but he kept the mirror turned face down and made no attempt to study himself in it. After a moment he gave the mirror and snapshot back to the clergyman. "I agree," he said. "I do look uncommonly like my ancestor."

The vicar sat heavily in his easy chair again. "The first Barnabas Collins was a most interesting person," he told them. "His history is clouded with omissions and opposing descriptions of both him and his times. But I do believe there was some unpleasantness which caused him to leave Collinsport and go to England."

Victoria glanced at Barnabas to see his reaction. The gaunt, handsome face was grim and a heavy vein at his temple seemed to throb. She had the impression he was restraining his impatience with difficulty.

He said, "I do not find myself as much interested in the story of the first Barnabas Collins as I am in the history of Stormcliff."

The vicar nodded pleasantly. "Stormcliff, of course! A fine old house built by the Collins family and sold to several owners. By a curious coincidence one of your own family, an English Collins, purchased the property shortly before it burned down in the early eighteen-seventies. As I recall he was also a Barnabas Collins, who had decided to return to this part of Maine for a while."

"I have heard him spoken of," Barnabas agreed.

"I have gone through a number of the letters and documents of that era," the old clergyman went on. "At the time of the fire a noblewoman from England was living at Stormcliff as a guest of your ancestor. I have come across references to the lady in a diary but I've never been able to discover her actual name. The entries in the diary refer to her as Lady C.D."

Victoria noticed a strange look come over the handsome, cadaverous features. Barnabas stared into the dying embers of the log fire with those hypnotic eyes and in a far-away manner murmured, "Lady Clare Duncan."

Lady Clare Duncan braced herself to remain primly seated upright in the shadowed interior of the jolting carriage. From outside the driver's loud imprecations mixed with the echoing of his horses' hooves on the rough cobblestones of the London street. Lady Clare had promised the driver a bonus if he managed to get her across the town to the flat of Barnabas Collins in a record time. The driver had agreed, even though the fog of this autumn night obscured the faint glimmer of street lamps and made the heavy traffic even more dangerous than usual.

He was certainly doing his best, although he might well kill both of them and wreck his carriage in the effort. Again the carriage swayed wildly as it rounded a corner to the driver's loud curse and the crack of a whip on the flanks of his team of grays. The small leather bag into which she'd gathered her most valuable jewelry and a large sum of money which she always kept handy for emergencies toppled from her lap and was lost in the darkness at her feet.

She groped for it anxiously, recovered it, and holding it firmly, resumed a sitting position. Barnabas had his lodgings over a pub in a rather poor section of the town. She'd only stopped by once before. And briefly at that. The handsome if somewhat gaunt young man had always been secretive about his personal life, and she had not wanted to seem prying. But after he'd declared his love for her, she'd insisted that he show her where he lived.

"It's a part of town frequented by theatre people, artists and other rogues," he'd told her with one of his grim smiles. "Not the kind of place for a young lady from a townhouse in Hyde Park."

"But I do want to see how you live," she'd pouted. She was twenty, blonde and lovely in a china doll way which belied her actual strength of character. Her wide blue eyes suggested innocence; she seldom let them reveal her shrewd mind. And the wealth she'd inherited from her late mother gave her an extra independence. She'd grown up not afraid to defy her father, the gouty Lord Augustus Duncan, who divided his time between the House of Lords and raising fine racehorses. It had been at Newmarket she'd first been introduced to Barnabas Collins by her father. She'd fallen in love with him at first sight though she'd concealed this well enough until it suited her to break the news to her father.

Lord Augustus had been so irate he'd hobbled up and down in front of her in the rich surroundings of the parlor of their fine town house. As he paced painfully back and forth his purplish face had been a picture of wrath.

"What do we really know about this man?" he demanded. "He's seen only rarely by most people. Occasionally he shows up at Newmarket and the other race courses and at the card tables of several fashionable clubs, but almost always alone. Who among our group are his friends?"

"He's only been in London a short time," she pointed out. "How could he have made many friends?"

"No excuse for him not knowing some of the right people," her father fumed. "I'll tell you who his companions mostly are! Theatre people, gamblers and scallywags! He roams London at night and vanishes during the day like the others in his underworld. How do you know he isn't some kind of criminal?"

"You have only to look at him to tell that," Lady Clare had said angrily. "He comes from a fine family. And he has independent means."

"And his lodgings are in the worst end of town!" Lord Augustus stood before her, a scowl on his florid face. "And if you need more, let me inform you tongues are wagging about him and the actress, Eileen O'Mara. And you know her reputation!"

Lady Clare indeed did know all about Eileen O'Mara. It was one of the reasons she had announced she wanted to marry Barnabas Collins. She feared the red-haired actress would win him first. Defiantly regarding her father, she said, "He doesn't love Eileen O'Mara and he does love me. And I'm going to marry him!"

"We'll see about that!" her father had warned her.

She'd taken it as mere bluster. What could he do, really? Disinherit her? She was independently wealthy already, through her mother's fortune. And so she had gone ahead with the great party for tonight, determined to have the engagement between Barnabas and herself announced.

Strangely, when she'd informed Barnabas of her plans, he'd shown a reluctance to rush things. With a worried air, he'd asked, "Why not allow me some extra time to win over your father?"

"We don't need to cater to him," she'd insisted as she rested snugly in his arms in the dark, shabby surroundings of his living room.

"There are other things to consider," he went on with his strong face shadowed. "My health is in a peculiar state. And while I am truly greatly attracted to you, I sometimes wonder if I should marry."

She had stared up into his hypnotic gray eyes. "Is there someone else? Do you love that actress, Eileen O'Mara?"

He shook his head. "I know her only as a friend. There was someone long ago back home. A girl named Josette. But she is forever lost to me."

Lady Clare had pressed close to him. "I shall make you forget your Josette," she'd promised. But he had still remained unconvinced about her plan that they should marry quickly.

Her father waited until tonight to play his trump card. He had come to her room before the party began on the pretext of admiring her dress. Elegant in tails and white tie himself, he had taken her hand and studied her with approval.

"You'll be the toast of London in that silver and white ball dress," he assured her. "All the young bloods will be at your feet."

"You're forgetting tonight is the night when Barnabas and I announce our engagement," she said with a carefree smile and whirled around lightly and curtseyed before him in her fancy gown. It had been a gesture which had pleased him from the days of her childhood.

But it did not please him now. "I think you are wrong in that," he said. "And to prove it, I have asked Barnabas Collins to join us here as soon as he arrives."

She stared at her father in disbelief. "But I must go downstairs to receive the early guests. The music will be striking up and Barnabas and I must have the first dance."

Her father looked grimly smug. "Those things can wait. Your aunt has undertaken to greet the early arrivals. This is more important."

Only then had she begun to feel afraid. She knew her father could be ruthless when he made up his mind. Had he concocted some fantastic plot against her beloved Barnabas?

"I refuse to believe anything you may say," she warned him.

"I'll leave it to your common sense, of which I'm sure there must still be a remnant left."

At that moment there had been a knock on the door and she'd opened it to reveal Barnabas in evening dress standing there. Over his formal dress suit he wore a black cloak lined with white satin. She thought he looked more handsome than ever. Yet his gaunt face showed a hint of concern and his eyes were fixed on her father as he entered the room.

"You asked to see me, sir?" Barnabas said, standing before her parent.

Lord Augustus was sneering. "Yes. I preferred to make certain charges against you in the presence of my daughter. It is my wish to let her know the sort of scoundrel you are."

Lady Clare at once rushed to Barnabas and angrily told her father, "You are wasting your time!"

"I think not," her father said with an assurance that made her uneasy.

Down below in the drawing room the music had begun. She raised her chin arrogantly and exclaimed, "Well, do get on with it! Barnabas and I want to dance."

"I doubt if you will," Lord Augustus said. And addressing himself to Barnabas he continued, "It has come to my attention that a week ago you were accused of cheating at cards at a certain prominent club which I shall not name."

Barnabas raised an eyebrow. "As you well know, Lord Duncan, that type of accusation is often made by a heavy loser at the gaming tables. It does not have to be true."

"I believe it was true in this instance," her parent said coldly. "You walked away from the accusation and refused to make any explanations."

"I was innocent," Barnabas maintained.

"You have not returned to the club. And if you do you will not be made welcome. Of course you realize that."

"This is ridiculous, father!" Lady Clare had protested. She took Barnabas by the arm. "I will hear no more of it."

Her father blocked their way as they attempted to leave. "There is something more," he said. "A matter concerning a young maidservant of this household whom this man has been furtively seeing while courting you."

Lady Clare had stared at her father in amazement. "Of course you are making that up!"

"It is the truth," her father said firmly. "And I can produce the girl and our housekeeper to prove it. Often when Collins leaves here he has picked up this girl and cavorted half the night with her. Several times the housekeeper has discovered her on the steps of the servants' quarters in a weak and fainting condition."

"This has to be a lie," she declared indignantly. "Tell him so, Barnabas!"

But Barnabas had stood there in silence with a stricken expression on his haunted yet handsome face. The veins at his temples bulged and his thick lips worked nervously.

"He can't deny it," her father said harshly. "Belle, the girl, has dragged his name into it and told of their assignations after his leaving here. Much of the time he abused her so that she had a partial loss of memory. And her throat is even now marked strangely from his cruel treatment of her."

She had felt her heart pound and nausea swell up in her.

Staring up at the pale Barnabas, she said, "Deny it!"

The gaunt face of the man she loved regarded her sadly. "I'm truly sorry, Clare," he said. "I'm unable to. I warned you there were things about me you did not understand. And that your plans for our marriage were premature." And with that he had turned and walked out of the room.

CHAPTER 2

Clare stood staring after him in consternation as he closed the door, leaving her alone with her father in the bedroom. It was a tragic ending to an evening she'd begun with so many hopes. All the music and gaiety in the big parlor downstairs meant nothing to her. She wouldn't have believed Barnabas capable of such deception.

Now her father came close to her and in a milder tone said, "Well, I hope you are satisfied."

She wheeled on him with her blue eyes blazing. "You are pleased that it has turned out this way, aren't you?"

His florid face took on an uncomfortable expression. "I was determined to protect you. You had to discover the truth before you became further involved with the scoundrel."

"I see," she said, barely controlling her fury.

"Now it is time to go downstairs and greet your guests," her father said as if it were all settled. "Your aunt has carried the burden long enough."

Clare eyed him defiantly. "I fear she will have to carry it for all the evening," she told him. "For I will not appear."

Her father's mouth dropped open. "What manner of nonsense is this?"

"I'm leaving this house and going to Barnabas," she declared. "And I shall beg him to marry me. On his terms."

"You're mad!" her father exclaimed.

"Mad or not, that is what I intend to do and you will not be able to stop me," she'd reminded him. It was a sore point between them that she had her own wealth and thus full independence.

Her father had ranted and raged but in the end he had left her to go downstairs and aid his sister in looking after the guests. Clare had then hurriedly changed from her elaborate evening gown to a brown taffeta traveling suit with a pert matching bonnet. Then she'd packed her jewelry and all her ready cash in the small leather bag and made her way downstairs by a rear stairway.

Reaching the street, she had hurried through the foggy darkness until she'd found a cabby willing to undertake the trip across town. He had seemed a surly, reckless type, suited to the challenge of driving her to Barnabas Collins' chambers in record time.

Now as she swayed back and forth in the dark, shabby carriage she was more than ever convinced that he was reckless and not so sure she had been wise in choosing him. But there was nothing to do but suffer the difficult situation through and trust she would soon reach the apartment over the pub in safety.

She tried to sort out her feelings and thoughts about Barnabas as a means of diverting her mind from the rough ride and the danger she was in. Until the moment when he had quietly admitted his being linked with the maidservant, Belle, she had accepted the story as one of her father's trumped-up falsehoods. But Barnabas had ended any doubts.

Recalling the maid, she remembered her as an exceptionally attractive dark girl, although not at all intelligent. She was too much given to blushes and giggling and Clare had often heard the housekeeper complain that the girl thought more about men than doing her work. And this was the silly young female Barnabas had chosen to use as a diversion. Clare found it impossible to believe that Barnabas could have taken Belle seriously. There must be another side to the story.

Perhaps the girl had turned to him for some sort of help. Barnabas had a warm heart. And before he knew it he'd become innocently involved with the comely dark-haired servant girl. It was an understandable situation and Clare felt she could easily forgive him for his lapse from faithfulness. Nor did she give much credence to the rumors which linked his name with that of the notorious actress, Eileen O'Mara. Again, she doubted a man of his character would find anything attractive about the flashy but disreputable actress.

She was ready to overlook any indiscretions Barnabas might have been guilty of in the past and start the slate clean. She loved him dearly and longed to be his wife. And she was reasonably sure that he returned her love, but because of his racy past had a bad conscience about asking her to marry him. She would make him realize he had no need to worry. If only she could get to his place ahead of him and be there waiting when he arrived. Ben, his manservant, would remember her and let her in to wait for his master.

The driver from his perch atop the carriage gave out with another resounding oath and called on his horses to halt. The carriage came to a jerking stop that hurled her forward. As she recovered herself and straightened her bonnet the driver pushed open the slot in the roof and told her they had arrived at their destination.

Then he got down and pulled open the door for her and helped her alight to the wet cobblestones of the grimy, narrow street. In spite of the drifting clouds of fog she recognized it as being the right spot. The lights from the pub under Barnabas' lodgings were pale and blurred by the London mist. She had the proper amount ready and pressed it into the hand of the cabman.

He checked the amount and stuffed the bills in his pocket. Then with an expression of cupidity on his dirty, unshaven face he touched a finger to his cap and said, "Thank'ee, miss. It's a bit rough hereabouts. Would you want me to wait to take you back?"

She was trembling from sheer nervousness but didn't want him to know that. Glancing around, she said, "I will make out nicely now. There'll be no need for you to remain. And thank you for making such good time."

"Cabs aren't easy come by here," he offered as a final warning.

"I have no intention of calling a cab," she informed him. "I plan to be living here."

Surprise quickly followed by disgust registered on his rough face. He clambered back to his perch on the carriage, flicked the reins with an oath and headed it clattering off into the misty darkness. As the creaking wheels and hoofbeats echoed in the distance she stood there feeling very much alone.

A woman's sudden scream from a second story on the opposite side of the street, followed by the harsh imprecations of a male voice, further terrified her. Then a window was raised and someone threw a vessel of slop out uncomfortably near. With a tiny whimper she scurried for the lights of the pub and tried to remember at which end of the building the entrance to Barnabas' second floor lodgings could be found.

Clutching the bag with her valuables tightly she sought the door while avoiding the pub. From inside the steamed windows of the pub issued sounds of hoarse hilarity and she suddenly had the fantastic impression of being the only sober person in a London wreathed in fog and enjoying a drunken brawl.

As she groped for the doorway and found none she made her way to the other end of the building. She'd only gone a few steps when a monstrous face presented itself close to her as it emerged from the mist—a grotesque twisted face with a huge drooping nose and a grinning toothless mouth. Madness showed in the creature's eyes and huge hairy hands reached out for her.

It was beyond endurance. She screamed and dodged quickly to one side. Hooting laughter rang in her ears as she at last reached the welcome safety of the sought-for doorway and stumbled up the dark, narrow steps. She prayed the ugly madman would not take it into his head to follow her, and when she reached the door of Barnabas' flat she pounded on it wildly and screamed to be let in.

In a minute the door was flung open. But it was neither Barnabas or his servant, Ben, who stood revealed there. It was the actress Eileen O'Mara.

The actress seemed fully as astonished as Clare was. Eileen O'Mara wore an orange dress of some showy material cut low to reveal the full line of her bosom. One hand rested on a hip as she regarded her with undisguised scorn.

"Lady Clare Duncan," she said. "So Barnabas has made another conquest. I've heard rumors about you, but until this moment I didn't believe them."

Clare's cheeks burned. She stiffened and tried to regain her poise. "Is Barnabas at home?"

The actress shook her head. "No. Just me and Ben. And Ben is drunk. Dead drunk."

This was upsetting news. But Clare could not retreat at this late moment. Forcing a casual tone, she said, "Then I must ask you to allow me to come in and wait for Barnabas."

"Why should I?"

"Because he will be angry with you if you don't," Clare bluffed.

Surprisingly, it worked. The hard, pretty face of the actress took on an acid smile. "Come in and wait if you like. I warn you it won't do you any good."

"Thank you," Clare said coldly, as she stepped inside still clutching the bag with her jewels and money. The dimly lighted living room seemed shabbier and smaller than it had before. From a dark passageway there came the sound of raucous snoring. That would undoubtedly be Ben.

Eileen O'Mara closed the door and came over beside her. "Barnabas belongs to me," she said. "You're wasting your time here."

Clare met her glance evenly. "We'll see about that."

The actress surveyed her with a sneer. "You may be Lady Clare and have half the money in London but you still won't get Barnabas for a husband."

Clare turned her back on the actress and in a dignified tone said, "I don't care to discuss that with you."

"You might be wise to," was the older woman's reply. "I'm not the only other girl in London Barnabas sees. He's a true lady-killer!" And here she laughed coarsely. "He's even been taking out one of your household servants on the sly."

Clare was so startled that she wheeled around again. "How do you know that?"

The redhead was triumphantly smiling. "I know a lot more about your Barnabas than most, dearie," she said.

Fear pierced through Clare again. She was beginning to believe Eileen. She had to, since the redhead obviously knew so much. "What else is there to know?" she asked in a small, taut voice.

"Plenty. And you'll be a lot safer for knowing it."

"What do you mean?"

Eileen O'Mara shrugged. "You probably won't thank me if I tell you. Or believe me either."

"If you have anything to say, say it before he comes."

The redhead looked smug. "You're curious now. Lady Clare Duncan. We're not so different, we women, even though we be born worlds apart. Have you ever heard of Josette?"

Clare frowned. Of course the name was familiar . . . Barnabas had mentioned a Josette as someone back home whom he'd loved, but who was forever lost to him now. "Yes. He has spoken to me of Josette."

"It is because you resemble her that he was drawn to you," Eileen O'Mara told her. "And it is that resemblance which kept him from using you as he has me and the others."

"What are you saying?"

"Barnabas only cares for you because you remind him of Josette. And it will do you no good. He's been searching for another Josette ever since she died years ago. And he's never found one. Angelique's curse has taken care of that."

Clare's mind was reeling. None of this made sense. "Who is Angelique and what is this nonsense about a curse?"

Eileen O'Mara laughed shortly. "You're a real innocent.

You don't know a thing, do you?"

The small, evilly-lighted room with its flickering tallow candle seemed like a fetid prison cell. Clare felt she might faint. On top of all the other happenings of the evening, this was too much. She sank into a rickety plain chair and stared up into the smug, smiling face of the redhead. "Tell me," she begged.

Eileen's eyes narrowed. "Barnabas values his privacy. He doesn't like anyone invading it. I had to bring a bottle of gin and get Ben dead drunk before he'd allow me to wait here for his master. I came here tonight to tell Barnabas I want money. Plenty of money, or I'll spread the truth about him all over London."

"What truth?"

The actress came close to her and turned her neck slightly. "Look at my throat."

Clare studied the shapely white throat and after a moment saw there was a weird red mark on it, like a bruise—but it was clearly not a bruise. She shuddered. "There is an odd abrasion there," she admitted.

The redhead faced her again. "Of course there is. And you'll find that same kind of mark on the throat of your housemaid, Belle. It's the mark Barnabas leaves."

"What madness is this?" she asked in a hushed voice.

"Not madness, but truth," the actress assured her. "Barnabas has an evil secret. It's strange you've never wondered about him. Why he doesn't ever show himself during the daylight hours?"

Clare's eyes widened. It was true. Barnabas only appeared after dusk set in. "What is the reason?"

"Because he is a special kind of man," Eileen O'Mara told her with relish. "He no longer is a human being like the rest of us. He is one of the living dead. He is a vampire who must have human blood to survive. That is why you see this mark on my throat and why there is a similar mark on your maid's. And the living dead walk only by night."

Clare was on her feet. "No! You're lying!"

The actress gripped her by both arms to subdue her hysteria and went on in an even voice. "Listen to me, for he will soon be here. Heed my warning. I'll let you hide somewhere to see and hear that I am right. Then, if you're lucky, he'll let you leave here alive. I can make no promise that he will."

Clare moaned. "I don't believe it! Barnabas is a fine man! I love him!"

"Little fool!" the actress snapped, still holding her by the arms. "Of course he was a fine man. But now he is a ghostly shell, a ghoul who sleeps in a coffin during the day and depends on Ben to look after him. A vampire who roams the streets of London at night for victims to appease his need for human blood, when Belle and I are not able to satisfy his thirst. Anyone he loves or who loves him is shadowed by the curse of Angelique. So make up your mind to forget him."

Clare couldn't allow herself to accept this. "You're making it all up," she insisted.

The actress smiled scornfully. "If I were, I wouldn't be here. He's made use of me. Now I'm going to blackmail him and make him pay well if I'm to keep his secret."

"He'll prove how wrong you are when he comes."

The redhead let go of her arms and studied her with a wry smile. "I'm willing to let it rest at that," she said.

"Watch when he stands in front of that wall mirror," she went on, pointing to the mirror on the opposite wall. "You'll see no reflection. The dead can not be seen in a mirror."

"It's too wild a story," Clare said.

"You'll see." The actress gave a small start and hurried to put her ear to the door. A frightened look crossed her coarsely pretty face and she came rushing back to Clare. Pushing her toward a nearby door, she said, "He's coming! Hide in that closet and leave the door enough ajar so you can tell what is going on in here."

She had no time for protest before she was shoved into the gloom of the dank-smelling closet. She hunched back to the rear of it but since Eileen O'Mara had left the door open a fraction she had a good view of at least half the room—the half in which the mirror was hung. She waited, hardly daring to breathe.

Now the rumbling of Ben's snoring was mingled with the sound of the door opening and heavy footsteps coming into the room. Eileen came to stand so that she could be seen through the narrow opening and Barnabas Collins moved over to face her.

"How did you get in here?" the gaunt, handsome man demanded in anger.

Eileen's lips curled in a smile. "I have persuasive ways. And Ben likes gin. I've been wanting to talk to you about something."

"We'll talk at my convenience," Barnabas said harshly. "You have no right being here. Get out!"

Eileen O'Mara didn't move. "I won't be ordered around by you any longer, Barnabas Collins," she said. "Now I'm going to make you pay."

Clare could see the astonishment on the solemn face of the man she wanted to marry. He rapped his silver-headed cane on the wooden floor as he glared at the actress. "What kind of talk is this?"

"I know what you are, Barnabas. And I've made up my mind to tell all London you're a vampire unless you pay me well for silence."

Clare watched Barnabas' reaction. He took it calmly enough.

He studied the actress grimly and said, "No one will listen to such a story."

"I'll chance that," the redhead said. "And we know it's so."

"It will be another matter proving it," Barnabas said with his expression more menacing than Clare had ever seen it.

But the actress didn't seem aware of the danger her words had thrust her into. She said, "You need my help, Barnabas. You no longer have Lady Clare."

"Leave her out of this!" Barnabas said with a vigor she would have applauded under other circumstances.

"You are finished in London if I don't remain quiet," Eileen O'Mara told him. "And you have so much money you'll never miss the little I want."

Barnabas appeared to be considering her words. He stared at her with his hypnotic eyes for a long moment. Then his mood seemed to soften. "Of course you are right," he agreed quietly. "I do need you, Eileen."

The redhead smiled. "Now you're making sense. You may be a vampire, Barnabas, but you're a charming one." He put aside his cane and moved closer to her, an imposing figure in his caped coat. He stood behind Eileen with his hands lightly around her waist. They were standing almost directly opposite the mirror and Clare's eyes naturally sought it. What she saw made her gasp and feel ill. The actress had been right. No reflection of Barnabas showed in the mirror although Eileen was plainly outlined there.

If Clare had any further doubts, this ended them. She was striving to grasp the enormity of it all and what it meant to her when she noticed that Barnabas had raised his hands and seemed about to grasp Eileen by the throat. Terror surged through her and she pressed a fist against her mouth to prevent herself from screaming out a warning to the redhead.

It happened in a flash. His hands cupped her throat and exerted a swift pressure on it. Eileen slumped and he bent over her neck, pressing his lips tightly against it.

Clare shut her eyes to the horror and doubled her hands until her fingernails bit into her palms, battling to keep from collapsing and betraying her presence at this awful moment. At last she opened her eyes again in time to see Barnabas lowering the body of the actress to the floor. He hesitated, staring down at her prone form with a look of revulsion on his gaunt face. And then he marched swiftly out of view and she heard him speaking loudly and angrily to his manservant.

A few minutes later he returned with a sleepy-eyed Ben dragging after him. Barnabas pointed to the body of Eileen on the floor. "She's done for this time," he said. "We've got to get away before she's missed or her body is discovered here."

Ben, a woefully heavy stooped man with sandy gray hair, regarded the body on the floor unhappily. "I had an idea she was out for trouble" he admitted.

Barnabas gave him an ugly glare. "And you were a fool to allow her to come in here."

Ben whined, "She said you were expecting her, sir."

"Which you knew to be a lie!"

"I couldn't be certain," the man faltered.

"She plied you with gin," Barnabas accused him angrily. "You can't be trusted where liquor is offered. Another mistake like this and you leave my service."

"Yes, sir." Ben bowed his head.

"Get rid of that creature's body," Barnabas ordered. "Put it in another room. The sight of it sickens me!"

He turned away wearily while Ben dragged Eileen's body across the floor and out of the room. When he was left alone, Barnabas began to pace up and down uneasily. Perspiration was flowing down his cheeks and Clare thought his skin had a strange pallor . . . the death shade of a corpse!

She watched the weird drama with terror in her lovely blue eyes. At any moment the door to the closet might be opened and her presence discovered. And despite the fact Barnabas had claimed to love her, she felt sure he would not hesitate to murder her as he had Eileen if he felt his secret was threatened with exposure. Scarcely daring to breathe, she waited to see what would take place next.

Ben came back into the room, still unsteady on his feet. "What now, sir?"

"We'll have to get out of London, you fool!" Barnabas said harshly, halting in his pacing. "You know what must be gotten ready. We'll take the Dover night train to France."

"Yes, sir," the servant said humbly. It was clear that he was afraid of Barnabas.

Clare held her breath, certain now that one or the other would approach the closet. A chill surged through her and her teeth began to chatter, even though the closet was dreadfully warm. She tried to decide what she felt toward Barnabas after all she'd discovered and was unable to come to any kind of conclusion. She had no idea what he would do if he discovered her there. She could only hope for some mercy.

He and the servant were engaged in packing a huge wooden case. And as they busied themselves with the task she heard Ben say, "I supposed you would still be at the Lady Clare's party. You must have left early?"

"That's finished!" Barnabas said abruptly, his back to the crack of the closet door as he bent over the case.

"A pity, sir," Ben ventured. "She was a lovely girl. So like Josette."

"No need to remind me of that," Barnabas said wearily. "I knew it wouldn't last. Her father discovered my relations with the maid, Belle. Of course I couldn't explain."

"Naturally not, sir," Ben said as he handed him a folded armful of clothing.

Barnabas straightened up again. "You can close and lock that case," he ordered Ben. "Now we'll take care of the casket. Do you have the bag with the Maine earth in it?"

"In the other room, sir," Ben said nervously.

"Be sure it is placed at my feet in the casket," Barnabas said severely. "You know I must always have Maine earth with me, the same earth in which I was buried."

"I know, sir."

"Then see you don't forget again," Barnabas told him as he strode over to another door and flung it open to reveal a coffin on a stand with lighted candles at its foot and head. Barnabas went on into the room, halting before the coffin.

Clare couldn't restrain a feeling of pity for the solitary figure standing by the casket, despite the murder she'd just witnessed. Eileen had, after all, been threatening to blackmail him, even though she knew he was the victim of an ancient curse: a vampire doomed to walk the earth apart from any real relationship with the world of the living, and forced to retreat to his coffin as soon as daybreak came. Surely Barnabas was to be pitied as well as feared.

But at the moment fear was the dominating emotion. As she watched, Ben joined the handsome gaunt man beside the coffin and waited with a respectful silence.

At last the servant said, "Are you ready, sir?"

Barnabas nodded. "It's time," he said. "It will be daylight long before we reach our destination. I must be prepared."

"I'll look after the transportation, sir," Ben promised. "I'll arrange it as soon as you're settled."

"Let there be no more mistakes," Barnabas warned him. "You know my powers and what your life will be worth if you fail me."

"No need to worry on that score, sir," Ben said nervously.

Barnabas silently climbed up into the coffin and lowered himself in it, as a normal person would retire on a bed. Clare watched it all from her place of concealment with horror registered on her lovely face. Next Ben found the lid of the coffin and placed it over the recumbent figure of Barnabas. He spent some minutes securing the lid in place with screws and then left the room. A few minutes later he made his way to the door of the flat and went down the stairs.

She waited until she was certain he was gone. Then she furtively emerged from the closet, in a nearly fainting condition. She had no idea where Ben had gone or how long he might be absent. But she felt reasonably sure she had at least a few minutes. She must leave before he returned or she'd be trapped.

Common sense dictated she flee at once. But curiosity made it impossible for her to leave without inspecting the weird bed of Barnabas Collins. The coffin into which she'd seen him calmly recline. Feeling it was all part of some nightmare, she approached the gray casket in the shadowed room and stared down at it. And all at once she was aware of a stirring under the closed lid!

CHAPTER 3

She shrank back from the closed coffin in horror. Wheeling, she fled from the room and the flat. Hurrying down the dark, uneven steps, she almost lost her balance but somehow she managed to save herself from falling and finally stepped out into the dismal fog of the mean street once again. For a moment she stood in the glow of the pub's lighted windows, not knowing which way to turn. Then she realized she must move on, Ben would surely soon be coming back.

Summoning her small remaining courage she forced herself to proceed along the narrow sidewalk past the pub and towards what she hoped might be a main street. The damp mist bit into her after the warm air of the flat and she trembled from cold as well as fear. Walking as swiftly as she dared in the almost impenetrable fog, she strained every sense, alert to the danger any unexpected sound or movement might mean for her.

She made her way along a narrow alley in which it would have been impossible for two to pass without brushing each other. Luckily no one appeared along the way. And now she had come to a wider street, but there was no hint of a light in any of the windows. The buildings displayed signs of merchants, tailors, greengrocers and other commercial firms—no wonder it was so deserted at this midnight hour.

Because of the fog and her confusion and fear, she had no

idea where she was heading. All she wanted to do was place as much distance between herself and the horror she'd witnessed at Barnabas Collins' flat as possible. She still clutched the leather bag with its valuable contents, knowing it made her a logical victim for theft or murder.

The mist swirled about her, blurring her vision as the terrifying memory of the events of the night fogged her mind. Now she came to an archway and with new fear rising up in her edged her way through its shadows. She had only gone a few steps when suddenly a figure loomed out of the darkness to block her way. Clare froze where she was and screamed.

" 'Ow, wot a ram go!" a voice young, female and coarse said in disgust. "I was sure you was some sport come along for a bit of fun!"

Just the sound of a human voice was reassuring. That it belonged to a young woman was also helpful. Clare breathed a deep sigh of relief. "I'm lost," she told the girl whose face or figure she could not see clearly because of the dark and fog.

"Lost you are!" the girl mocked her. "And a la-de-da lady by the sound of you. The streets are no place for your sort at this hour."

Clare improvised hurriedly. "I came down here to visit a sick friend. I haven't been able to find a cab to take me home. You must know the area. If you can get me transportation I'll reward you with a pound."

"A pound!" The girl's tone registered awe and astonishment. "You're a whole lot better prospect than any sport. Come along!" And with that she turned and led the way through the arch and into another narrow street.

"I'm so glad I found you," Clare said gratefully as she walked along beside the girl.

"Not half so glad as me, dearie," her new companion said cheerfully. "There's a pub called the Bull and Bear not more than a block away. Hansom cabs are always bringing swells there at every hour of the night. Sports out to do the town, if you know what I mean. I had myself a bit of an argument in the ladies' parlor with someone no better than she ought to be a fortnight ago and I've stayed away since. But I'll take you there now and you'll have yourself a hansom in two shakes."

Within minutes they were standing before a brightly lighted pub from which the sound of accordion music and boisterous hilarity issued. And shortly after that a cab deposited two stout males in evening clothes, top hats and opera cloaks on the sidewalk near Clare and the girl. At once the men winked and leered at them.

But the girl was a match for the amorous, drunken pair. "On into the pub, you gents," she told them. "Me and my friend will come in after."

With assurances they would be waiting, the men weaved their way into the pub while the girl hurriedly led Clare to the cab. The driver glared down at them.

"Just a minute, you two!" he said harshly. "I'm taking no such fares until I see the color of your money!"

"I can pay!" Clare said anxiously, staring up at his angry face.

"Cor!" the girl cried in disgust. "Can't you see she's a toff? Wot you want to do? Lose out on a good thing?"

The cabby looked slightly more interested but he insisted, "Let me see you have enough cash first, miss." Clare opened the leather bag and brought out a handful of banknotes. "You have no need to worry," she assured him.

"All right," he said grudgingly. "Get in."

Clare quickly turned to the girl, who she saw now was pretty in a forlorn, bedraggled way. "Thank you, so much," she said. And gave her several pound notes.

The girl again registered surprise. "You said one!"

"It's worth more to me," Clare smiled. "Bless you!"

"Bless you, my lady," the girl said in her cheerful way as she thrust the bills down her bosom and then waved goodbye to Clare who had gotten into the cab.

The driver opened the slot and glared down at her. "Where to?"

This made her momentarily tongue-tied. She hadn't thought where she'd go. Certainly she didn't want to return home and face her angry father. She needed a refuge to consider her problems and decide what to do. But where? All at once she thought of Aunt Flo. The old lady was her mother's aunt and the lone survivor of that generation of her family. She lived in regal splendor in a mansion in Mayfair with a retinue of servants. And she had always been fond of her. The admirable spinster was the logical one to turn to in this crisis.

"It's in Mayfair," she told the driver. And gave him her aunt's address. He looked astonished and dubious but slammed the slot shut and got the cab underway.

So once again she was being trundled over the cobblestoned streets of London, this time at a much more sober pace and in a much more sober frame of mind. The dream of marriage with Barnabas Collins had turned into a nightmare. She still could not fully accept what she had seen and heard in that shadowed flat. It was too incredible! Surely it had been a weirdly staged prank to terrify her.

But there were overtones to it all which chilled her spine. She realized now that in spite of his gaunt, handsome face and great charm there had always been something strange about Barnabas. He had truly been a man of mystery. She had never seen him before dusk. Was he a vampire, cursed by some jealous female to live on for centuries as one of the walking dead? Doomed never to love truly or be loved ever again, forced to find victims to supply him with the blood he required for even this nebulous existence?

Eileen O'Mara had been one of those whose blood he had drank. And so had the pretty servant girl, Belle. But Barnabas had never attempted to feast on her blood, Clare thought with a shudder. Perhaps he had truly loved her and had hoped that they might one day be man and wife. She wanted to believe that.

Barnabas was doomed and pitiful—yet there was a ruthless side to his nature as well. Faced with greed and the threat of exposure, he had turned on Eileen in a rage and drained her of blood until she was dead. Clare still felt ill at the memory of what she'd seen. But even then Barnabas had shown himself not to be the complete villain her father pictured him. Immediately after Eileen's demise he had shown remorse. The murder had been a hasty act of self-preservation in which he'd found no satisfaction.

As the cab rolled on through the fog-ridden streets towards Mayfair she determined what she would tell Aunt Flo. It would be hopeless to try and explain the vampire business to the old lady. She would no more accept the story than she would that of a witch on a broomstick. So Clare knew she must keep it strictly to an account of an unfortunate love affair. She would not even name Barnabas. Simply inform her aunt she and her father had quarreled over her choice of husband and that she had then been jilted by the young man. As she recalled, Aunt Flo had once been through the same ordeal in her young days.

Aunt Flo listened to Clare's version of the night's events and at once placed an arm around her in sympathy. "I'm so happy that you came to me in your time of distress," the white-haired, stout old lady said sympathetically. "I know exactly how you must feel. I was jilted ages ago by the most wonderful young man. He ran off with an Italian shrew who gave him a wretched life. Poor thing!"

Clare smiled. "I felt you were the only person who would understand," she told the old woman. "It is so kind of you to take me in." She had arrived at her aunt's mansion in the small hours of the morning and roused the servants with difficulty. But once Aunt

Flo knew who it was she'd risen from her bed and come down to greet her warmly.

"You may stay with me as long as you like," Aunt Flo assured her. "And that father of yours had better not try to come here pestering you or I'll have the servants show him the door."

And thus began a month's stay in the mansion in Mayfair. Aunt Flo, who reminded Clare of a stout old tabby cat in a lace cap, was a gracious hostess. But it was a very quiet household; even the servants were in their seventies. Clare was left with little to do but read and sit or stroll in the garden with her aunt on warm days. Aunt Flo loved to crochet and was rarely without her crochet needles and some project in her lap.

After a fortnight Clare became uneasy in the sedate atmosphere of the house. Also, she was beginning to have second thoughts about Barnabas. The newspapers had carried an account of Eileen O'Mara's dead body being found in an alley near the pub over which Barnabas had his flat. It read that the police had no reason to suspect violence though a peculiar red mark had been found on her throat and her body seemed to be almost completely without blood. The verdict finally rendered was that the actress had died of unknown natural causes.

So Barnabas would not have the murder over his head! But what would he do in France? She had heard him instruct Ben to book passage for them on the Dover Calais boat train. And she found herself longing to see and talk with him again. The love she had known for Barnabas had not been completely crushed. Indeed, it had become a deeper and perhaps less romantic emotion with her. Now she began to think he needed her and her love to salvage him from the desolation of the curse. Knowing that she was aware of the terrifying truth about him and still able to love him might change his entire outlook on life. Perhaps would even be effective in destroying the curse and make him once again a normal man.

The more she thought about this the more it appealed to her. Perhaps it was too optimistic and foolhardy on her part to want to follow Barnabas and try to help him. But she had never been known for her discretion and the thrill it offered was an extra inducement. She began to make plans about how she would manage her pursuit. She hesitated to set out on the expedition alone, but she could only have a companion who would have some understanding of her predicament and be sympathetic to it, someone who would feel the same way she did about Barnabas Collins.

Almost at once a name presented itself to her. Belle! She had not known the maid well other than to notice that she was a pretty, rather shallow girl. But Belle had known Barnabas and been one of those who supplied him with blood. Belle might still be infatuated with him and willing to try and help him.

With this in mind she despatched one of Aunt Flo's elderly manservants with a message for the girl and an invitation for her to come to Mayfair for a meeting.

A nervous Belle presented herself the following afternoon, looking deliciously lovely and young in a pale blue dress which matched her dark hair and complexion and wearing a bonnet with dangling blue ribbons. Clare took her out to the garden so they could talk without being overheard.

She at once tried to put the shy girl at ease by saying, "I am your friend, Belle. And I know that you met Mr. Barnabas Collins and liked him."

Belle twisted her hands nervously in her lap. "We were never proper friends, miss. But he took me on moonlight walks and he was a wonderful one to talk. He told me stories about America and places I have only heard of."

"I understand," she said quietly. "You realize Barnabas and I were engaged and he suddenly broke it off and went away."

"Yes, miss." Belle kept her eyes cast down.

"I bear you no malice for that. Barnabas did it because he is in great trouble. I would like to help him so I plan to follow him to France. I need a companion with me and I thought of you. I'm sure you still have a fondness for him."

The girl looked up at her, blushing furiously. "Indeed, I do, miss. Not that I would ever expect a man like Mister Barnabas to marry a girl like me. But it was wonderful to have his friendship."

Clare was touched by the girl's sincerity. She studied her with grave eyes. "I find that commendable in you, Belle. You must try to understand that Barnabas is not a well man." She paused significantly. "I believe that he sometimes kissed you. Kissed you on the throat."

Belle stared down at her clasped hands again. "Yes, my lady," she said nervously. "But I have little remembrance of those times. My mind seemed to fog and I would recall only that we'd been together. It was strange."

"You mustn't worry about it," Clare told the girl. "And if you agree to journey to France with me in search of Barnabas I guarantee no harm will come to you. And I will pay you handsomely."

The girl looked up with an almost eager expression on her attractive oval face. "I would like to go with you, my lady. I'm most anxious to be of help."

So it was settled. Clare arranged with the girl to join Aunt Flo's household the first of the following week. And as soon after that as possible she would arrange passage for them to France. The first stop would be Calais where she would try to pick up some clue as to where Barnabas and his servant had gone.

As she feared, sending the message to Belle betrayed her hiding place to her father. Lord Augustus had sent a lad to follow Belle to the house in Mayfair. And that very evening he presented himself in the drawing room of Aunt Flo's mansion before the old woman and Clare.

Hands clasped behind his back, his weight on one leg to favor the gouty member, he stood before the fireplace glaring at them.

"I am willing to forgive all if you will return home," he told Clare.

She met his gaze calmly. "I'm sorry. Father," she said. "I have decided on a holiday in France. Perhaps after I return I'll come home to you."

Her father's florid face registered rage. "And you want that Belle to go with you. Don't think I'm not aware what that means. You're going to meet that blackguard Collins!"

Aunt Flo paused in her crocheting to mildly reprove Lord Duncan. "I beg you to control your temper, Augustus," she said. "These angry exhibitions must worsen your gout."

"I can take care of my gout, madam," Lord Duncan said with biting sarcasm. "Just so long as you don't try to turn my daughter against me."

"Nothing is further from my intentions," the old woman assured him as she resumed her needlework.

Clare's father turned his attention to her again. "I hope you are aware of the danger you place yourself in following that scoundrel to the Continent. There are some nasty stories going around the town about him."

She smiled sweetly. "I'm sure there are and that you are one of those keeping them in circulation. It's no use, father. I'm going to have my holiday and there's nothing you can do about it."

"We'll see about that!" Angrily he stomped out. Because of his threatening attitude Clare rushed her plans to travel. She was certain her father would make some attempt to prevent her leaving London. He might even go so far as to plead she was insane and have her confined for her own good. So as soon as Belle arrived in Mayfair the packing for the trip began. And on the Wednesday night of that same week the two young women boarded the boat train for Calais.

The first few days on French soil were full of frustration. No one seemed to remember seeing Barnabas Collins and his servant. And Clare began to fear they had never made the journey.

Then, quite by accident, she and Belle stopped at a small inn on the outskirts of the town for dinner. And when she presented the usual queries about Barnabas the face of the elderly innkeeper lit up.

"Oui, mam'selle," he said. "He was here and my guest. The sick gentleman who carried his coffin along with him. A macabre idea, is it not?"

"When did they leave?"

"They remained here until ten days ago, mam'selle," the old man said. He frowned. "The thin one, the servant, told me his master was becoming resdess. A strange man, indeed. Only after dinner did he present himself. All day long he remained in his room. According to the servant this man was going to Mont St. Michel to consult a Dr. Fontaine."

Clare frowned. "Mont St. Michel. I do not know it."

"It is a small place," the innkeeper told her. "The great Gothic abbey the 'Marvel' is its claim to fame. Built on a rocky island that connects with the mainland at low tide only. There is a small village and many people climb the nine hundred steps from the base to the roof of the Benedictine Monastery for the incomparable view."

She said, "And this Dr. Fontaine lives there."

"According to the servant, Ben," the innkeeper said. "It is a strange lonely place for a doctor to live, that island." He shrugged. "But then it is a strange world, is it not, mam'selle?"

"Indeed it is," she agreed. "And you feel sure that is where Mr. Collins has gone?"

"Quite sure," the innkeeper said. "The coffin went with them when they left by stage one midnight."

"Will I be able to find lodgings on this island of Mont St. Michel?" she asked.

The innkeeper nodded. "Yes. The village has only a single street but there are several inns and eating places. The monastery is deserted but it makes a magnificent monument."

"Thank you," Clare said. When she and Belle were alone at the table Clare told the maid, "Perhaps we can reach Mont St. Michel in time to catch up with them."

Belle looked pleased. "Yes, my lady."

They took the stage to the junction between Normandy and Brittany where Mont St. Michel was located. And as soon as it was low tide they went out to the lonely, rocky island, jealousy guarded by the sea except for a few hours in every twenty-four. Both she and Belle were weary from their journey and happy to register at the best of the island's hotels, which was only a simple, tiny inn.

During the ride to Mont St. Michel they had been

fascinated and more than a little awed by the spectral edifice towering over the island and the surrounding ocean. The high monastery gave the island an eerie look. Its great fortified heights which dated back to the thirteenth century had an ominous, forbidding air. Clare hoped this was only an impression and had no meaning for their journey.

Following her usual custom she asked about Barnabas Collins at the inn but no one there seemed to have seen him. And then she inquired where Dr. Fontaine lived. The reaction to this question was startling.

The stout hotel proprietor frowned at her. "You know Dr. Fontaine?"

"No. But I have a friend who does. I'm anxious to meet him."

"His house is beyond the village on a hill, mam'selle," the innkeeper said curtly.

"Could I hire someone to take me to it?" she suggested.

The innkeeper shook his head. "I doubt it, mam'selle. No one on the island goes near the place. It has an evil reputation."

"An evil reputation?"

"Dr. Henri Fontaine is a sinister man engaged in dark experiments," the stout man said earnestly. "We are a simple people. We do not pry. But men and women who have ventured up there have not been seen again. I can only warn you, mam'selle."

Clare felt she understood. If Dr. Fontaine's patients suffered the kind of affliction Barnabas Collins did, it was understandable he should desire a great deal of secrecy. And such patients would arrive and depart under cover of darkness. Certainly the doctor could be accused of conducting weird experiments, but if this was for the purpose of helping unfortunates like Barnabas he was to be commended.

She thanked the innkeeper, deciding that she would make the trip up to the home of Dr. Henri Fontaine on her own. Leaving the hotel early in the morning of her first day on the island, she got some detailed instructions about finding the house from a small boy. She thanked him and he watched her go with a strange expression on his young face. Even the children of the island had been infected with the fear for the doctor.

After she left the town she climbed a steep, rocky road and followed a path to the left which led directly to a stone, castle-like structure built overlooking the sea. To all appearances the place was deserted but she knew this could not be so. When she reached the stout oaken entrance door she rapped on it, expecting someone would come to let her in. But no one did.

There wasn't a sound but the wash of the waves on the

rocks at the bottom of the cliff. Nor was there a sign of anyone moving about the grounds. Perhaps the boy had not given her the proper instructions—and yet this was exactly like the place described by the innkeeper. She left the door and stared at the shuttered windows. Then she walked around to the back where there was a garden. The flowers matched the rainbow in their colors and were of the low-lying rock garden variety. She was admiring them when she heard a footstep on the gravel walk and turned to see a slim, flaxen-haired young woman of great beauty studying her from the distance of a few feet.

Clare managed a smile. "I'm looking for Dr. Fontaine," she said.

The slim beauty wore a black velvet dress with a high collar covering her throat. A single strand of pearls relieved the starkness of her dress. In perfect English, she asked, "Who are you?"

"I'm a friend of Barnabas Collins," Clare said.

The flaxen-haired woman stared at her in silence a moment. Then she said, "Did he send you here?"

"In a way," Clare hedged. "I'm very anxious to talk with Dr. Fontaine and Barnabas as well. Is he still here?"

"You'll have to discuss that with the doctor," the woman said, not taking her eyes from her.

"When can I meet him?"

"Not until after dinner," the woman said. "He is busy in his laboratory during the day and must not be interrupted."

"Can I call on him this evening?" she wanted to know. "I'm staying in the village with my maid."

"He will let you know," the woman in black told her. "Let me have the name of your hotel."

Clare gave it to her and added, "I'm Lady Clare Duncan. If the doctor gives my name to Barnabas I'm positive he will see me."

"I will tell the doctor." The woman's lovely face showed no expression. And she stood there waiting for Clare to leave.

She couldn't help feeling like an intruder. "I'm sorry to bother you," she apologized. "I'll wait for the doctor's message."

At seven that evening a village lad brought an envelope and left it with the innkeeper. Clare opened it eagerly and found a single sheet inside with a message in ink written in a neat hand: "Dear Lady Clare Duncan, Thank you for contacting me. Welcome to our tiny island. My wife and I would like to have you as our guest. Come and bring your maid along as well. I have some information regarding our mutual friend, Barnabas Collins. Sincerely, Henri Fontaine."

Clare was at once eager to transfer from the hotel to the stone castle by the sea. But she was confronted with a problem.

Who would move her? She took this up with the innkeeper.

The stout man scratched his thick head of gray hair. "You'll need a carriage for your luggage," he said. "And I don't know anyone who would want to go up there. And especially not after dusk."

"There's still some time before dusk will set in," she said. "Surely there must be someone."

The innkeeper frowned and considered. At last he said, "There is Peter, the half-wit, who has a donkey cart. I suppose that would get you there, mam'selle."

"Anything will do," she said.

Less than an hour later, she and Belle were seated in the donkey cart which also carried their luggage and making the short trip to Dr. Fontaine's isolated home. Peter presided over his donkey and made no attempt at conversation. And when they reached the entrance to the house he quickly unloaded their bags, took the money Clare had agreed to pay him, and drove off quickly without a word.

Again Clare rapped on the door and hoped that this time it would be opened to her. It was. A moment later it swung wide to reveal a thin old man in shabby livery.

She told him, "It's Lady Clare Duncan and her companion."

The old man nodded wearily. "Yes, Lady Duncan. You are to come in and wait for the doctor in the parlor."

Turning, she indicated her luggage still on the steps. "What about these?"

"I'll look after them, My Lady," the old man said, standing back so she and Belle could enter.

The inner hall was as dark and gloomy as the exterior had suggested. Clare felt it was an unusual place for a doctor to have a private hospital—but then, his was an unusual practice.

There was a musty air of dank age about the old house which spoke of abandonment and neglect, although Dr. Fontaine must do his chief work there. Clare glanced around at the peeling walls and the heavy purple curtains which seemed to suggest mildew. And again she noticed the deathly silence.

Belle stood beside her, taking in her surroundings with anxious eyes. Clare had found the girl a pleasant but silent companion. She talked seldom, unless directly addressed, and seemed to be daydreaming a good deal of the time.

Now the purple curtains masking the entrance to a side room parted and the young woman in black came out followed by a tall, smiling older man, also dressed in black. He said, "I'm Dr. Henri Fontaine and this is my wife, Madeline. We are delighted to welcome you to our home."

Clare studied him with deep interest. His face was thin and strong with a high-bridged nose and peculiarly arched nostrils. His hair was white and thinning but his eyebrows were a startling black and almost met above the thin nose. His mouth, beneath a neat white mustache, was rather cruel looking and his ears were an odd pale color and pointed somewhat at the tops.

He came forward and extended his hand to Clare. "Barnabas did not warn me what a beauty you were, Lady Duncan," he said unctuously. His hand closed on hers and she winced as she found it to be icy cold!

CHAPTER 4

Attempting to hide the revulsion she felt at the clammy coldness of his handshake, she quickly introduced the doctor and his wife to Belle. The doctor seemed to show a special interest in the pretty servant girl and held her hand for a noticeably long moment. His wife, Madeline, maintained her cold reserve.

The ancient servant appeared with their bags and Dr. Fontaine directed him to take them upstairs and show them their rooms. He smiled at Clare as she started to follow the manservant. "You'll join us for a sherry in the living room after you're settled, I trust."

She nodded. "I would enjoy that. Is Barnabas still here with you?"

"No," Dr. Fontaine said. "But I expect he'll be returning within a few days. Until then I'll be honored to have you as our guest."

"Thank you," she said and joined Belle on the stairs behind the servant carrying their bags.

The old man led them down a murky corridor with an enormously high ceiling. He stopped by an open door and gestured for Clare to enter. She found herself in a large bedroom equipped with fine pieces of furniture including a canopied bed. The servant deposited the bags by the foot of the bed and then moved to another door to the left of the big bed and opened it. Clare glanced through the doorway and saw that it was a smaller room with an iron bed and few other items of shabby furniture. This was plainly to be Belle's room.

With this taken care of, the old man bowed once again and left without ever having said a word to them. It was a strange house with even stranger people.

Clare glanced about at the lavish, if dusty, furnishings of the room. The walls were heavy with grime and the carpets were thick with dust.

Noticing that Belle also seemed to be surprised by the air of neglect which was apparent everywhere in the house she told the girl, "I imagine the doctor and his wife are so occupied with his hospital work they have little interest in the rest of the place."

"Yes, my lady," Belle said in her usual colorless fashion.

"You may unpack and then go to bed," Clare told her. "I'll freshen up a little and join the doctor and his wife downstairs. I must find out more about Barnabas."

A few minutes later she advanced slowly down the stairs to the dimly lighted lower hallway. Dr. Fontaine had not made it clear which room was the drawing room. She hesitated in the hallway, hoping to hear some sound of voices to give her a clue. But the silence which seemed a characteristic of the old house prevailed once more. Tentatively she advanced to the purple drapes and pushed one aside. The stench of damp and dust assailed her nostrils and the drape felt grimy to her touch.

Revealed to her was a huge gloomy drawing room with high ceiling and a great dominating crystal chandelier thick with dust and cobwebs. The only light came from a roaring log fire in the wide stone fireplace at the end of the room. Silhouetted there against the flames were the slim, silent figures of her host and hostess.

Dr. Henri Fontaine strode forward to meet her. "We've been anticipating your joining us," he said with one of his thin smiles. "I suppose you find the house in a dreadful state of repair. You must forgive us. We have not had time recently to give it much attention."

"No doubt your work is demanding," she said, taking in some other details of the cavernous room. The flickering glow from the fireplace highlighted various aspects of it, one instant revealing a cobwebbed and dust covered mirror and then a sideboard whose silver was black with tarnish.

Dr. Fontaine took her by the arm and led her down nearer the fire where his wife, Madeline, stood staring longingly into the red, yellow and blue of the flaming logs. "Madeline is fond of the fireplace," he said. "She is always complaining of the cold, while I do not mind it at all."

Clare said, "I suppose a great old house like this so near the sea is bound to be damp."

"You are quite right," Dr. Fontaine said in his clipped British accent. "Perhaps you are surprised that my wife and myself speak English so well."

"I had not expected it," Clare admitted.

The doctor's sallow face showed another smile. "The truth is, we spent a long period in London and had a fine opportunity to perfect our mastery of your difficult language."

"My own French is so weak," Clare apologized. "It is fortunate for me that you are so fluent. Are many of you patients English?"

A gleam came into his oddly bright eyes. "I draw my patients from all over the world. There are few people trained in my specialty."

"I don't quite understand what your specialty is," she was quick to say. "But I know Barnabas is in terrible trouble and if he came to you for help you must be aware of his condition."

"Barnabas Collins presents a most interesting problem," the old doctor said suavely. "Don't you agree, Madeline?" The last words were spoken sharply as if in reprimand.

His beautiful young wife turned quickly from her study of the flames. "I always am in agreement with you, Henri."

His smile was sarcastic. "A dutiful wife." He turned to Clare again and asked, "Just how well are you acquainted with the state of Barnabas Collins' health?"

She found herself unable to speak bluntly of the horror that was so firmly etched on her mind. The events in the flat that dreadful night in London. She managed, "His illness is so unique and repulsive I hesitate to speak of it."

The doctor's heavy black eyebrows arched. "Lady Duncan, you are a most sensitive person. And I am one who appreciates sensitivity. There is no need to spell out what is wrong with Barnabas, since we both are aware of it."

Clare was grateful. There was a slight tremor in her voice as she asked him, "Is there any hope that he may be cured, Doctor?"

The deep-set eyes of Dr. Fontaine were fixed on her intently. "You are in love with him, aren't you?"

"Yes," she said in a small voice. "I have tried to persuade myself that it is useless, that I should put him out of my thoughts. But I have not succeeded."

He nodded in an understanding way. "Do not worry. It will work out happily for you both. I promise you I'll see to that."

Clare offered him a timid smile. "You can't know how relieved I am to hear you say that. How long before Barnabas will return?"

"A matter of a few days," Dr. Fontaine said casually. "And now we must enjoy the sherry I promised you." He moved a few steps to a low table on which there were two decanters along with several wine glasses. He lifted one of the decanters and filled two of the glasses carefully then advanced toward her and his wife with a glass in each hand. "You and Madeline shall have the sherry." He smiled and handed them the well-filled glasses.

Clare said, "Aren't you joining us?"

"Most certainly," he said. "But I prefer a different vintage, one which I doubt either of you would appreciate or even enjoy." He was back at the table filling a good-sized goblet with a ruby red liquid from the other decanter. When he'd finished he raised the goblet and said, "Let us drink to the success of my project."

The log fire was burning low now and the great gloomy room was more shadowed than before. Clare shivered slightly as she sipped the excellent sherry and found it warming. While she was grateful that Barnabas had discovered someone ready to help him, she could not ignore the gray-haired doctor's oddness. Nor could she quite understand the melancholy attitude and silence of his wife.

Glancing up, she saw that Madeline was staring at her in what seemed a fascinated incredulity.

Clare forced herself to smile and say, "It is most kind of you to have me as your guest."

Madeline's eyes remained fixed on her. "I carry out my husband's wishes."

Dr. Fontaine moved in quickly to say, "My wife is a very shy person. You must forgive her. We both want you to be happy here. And I'm impressed by the beauty of your little maid. Has she any idea of the purpose of your journey?"

"In a sense," Clare said. "I haven't told her everything. But it may interest you to know that she was one of those whom Barnabas preyed on."

"That does interest me," Dr. Fontaine said with a satisfied expression on his aquiline face. "Every detail helps." He took another drink from the goblet which he'd almost emptied.

There was something about the color and consistency of the bright red wine he was drinking which startled her. The liquid resembled blood more than it did wine. But she put this thought down to a vivid imagination and her associating the doctor with Barnabas' plight. And she dismissed the foolish notion at once.

"I would like to gain some understanding of your work," she told him.

Dr. Fontaine looked pleased. "You shall. I promise you that. I intend to have you visit my work quarters in the cellar. Perhaps tomorrow."

"I should like that."

He smiled. "You may find my methods unorthodox . . . but

then, I'm dealing in an unorthodox field. At the moment I'm without any helpers. Madeline assists me but I have no one else. I may even enlist your services while you are here."

Clare said, "I'll be glad to do anything I can while Barnabas is a patient."

"Most kind of you," he said and drained the goblet.

"Can you not get help from the village and train them?" she asked.

He shook his head. "They are an ignorant, superstitious lot. I've not even been able to get household servants from among them. Drale, the old man who looked after your bags, is a former patient of mine and the only servant we have in this large place. So you can understand why things are so badly in need of care." He gestured around the room with a hand.

Clare felt sorry for him. "It's too bad," she said. "I know the village people have taken the wrong meaning from your experiments. They all warned me against coming up here."

"Typical," Dr. Fontaine said with a hint of anger in his tone.

"I tried to tell them they were wrong, but they wouldn't listen," she said.

"Madeline cannot get anyone to help her when she buys supplies in the village. She has to carry them back by herself. I have Drale meet her at the half-way point, but it is a nuisance."

As she listened to him it was suddenly apparent to her that they were standing in almost total darkness. Only a tiny glow of light came from the dying logs. And she could no longer clearly make out Madeline's figure. Even the doctor, who was standing by her, was blurred to her eyes.

She finished her sherry and apologized, "I have kept you too long. It is time to retire for the night."

Dr. Fontaine took her empty glass. "You must be tired," he said. "I'll see you to the stairs." And he led her across the dark room after she'd said goodnight to a Madeline lost somewhere in the shadows.

At the stairs he said, "Drale will bring your meals to your room. We have not used the dining room down here for some time. It is more convenient this way. And do not expect to see much of us during the day, although Madeline may find time to show you around. Tomorrow evening I may decide to let you see what I'm doing in the cellar."

"Don't forget my offer to assist you," she begged. "I do want to contribute something after all you are doing for Barnabas."

He took her hand in his and again she was made uneasy by the clammy coldness of his grasp. "Never fear," he said. "I shall find some useful task for you. And perhaps for your maid as well."

"She is willing and obedient," she promised. Then they said their goodnights and she went on up to her room.

Belle had lighted a candle and set it on the bedside table for her return. By the soft candlelight the big, high-ceilinged room did not seem so completely neglected. The dust and grime did not show in the same manner as in daylight. Even the windows did not reveal their dirty condition with a full moon streaming in through them.

Clare moved closer to one of the windows and stared out at the sea and the reflected silver of the moonlight on the water. Only the crash of distant waves broke the silence. And yet there was something in the atmosphere here which made her uneasy. Something she could not understand.

Her thoughts were suddenly interrupted by a long unearthly wail rising from the lower regions of the castle-like mansion. It was sustained for a shattering moment and then quickly ended. She turned toward the door leading to the corridor, a startled expression on her attractive face. She listened, but now there was only silence. She tried to reassure herself that the cry might have come from a wild animal roaming outside the house, or perhaps some tortured patient whom Dr. Fontaine was trying to help.

She continued to stand there apprehensively rather than prepare for bed. And then on a sudden impulse she crossed to the door leading to Belle's room and opened it. The pretty servant girl was sleeping peacefully. Somehow the sight eased her tension. Gently closing the door, Clare returned to her own bedside and began to undress.

Long after she'd snuffed out the candle she continued to stare up from her pillow with wide-awake eyes. Her thoughts were chiefly of Barnabas and the tortuous journeying she'd done to follow him. Now on this lonely island they would meet again. And Dr. Fontaine had promised he would make it possible for their love to be fulfilled in a normal way.

When Barnabas returned in a few days she would be there to meet him and tell him of the love she felt for him—a love so great that it fought against the reality of his being one of the living dead. And that love would sustain him through Dr. Fontaine's treatments, whatever they might be, and restore him to her as a whole man again. The curse of Angelique would be removed and they would live together happily as man and wife.

It was with this warm hope for the future that Clare at last closed her eyes and dropped off to sleep. It was a dreamless sleep, but it was not destined to last long. She was awakened by a soft flapping against one of the windows. At first she was not completely awake and unable to focus on what the disturbance was. But, as she raised herself on an elbow and stared at the window with frightened eyes, she saw that it was a large bat striking against the window panes again and again in a vain attempt to burst into the room.

The macabre night creature vanished for a moment and then repeated the assault again. Terrified that it might finally break through into the room, Clare was on the point of getting out of bed and rousing Belle. But once again it flew off into the darkness and this time it didn't return.

Clare lay back on her pillow wondering what it signified. Could it be some sort of warning? A harbinger of evil to come? Had something happened to Barnabas? He was always in great danger because of his thirst for blood and the dire lengths to which it could carry him. Dr. Fontaine had said Barnabas had gone away for a few days . . . but he hadn't explained why. Nor where. What could have been the reason for his leaving in the middle of his treatments?

She lay tossing restlessly in her bed. The moonlight no longer shone so strongly through the windows but there was still enough light for her to see the details of the room with ease. More than a half-hour went by and she was about to touch a light to the candle and give up any idea of sleep when she was startled by a creaking sound from the corridor outside her room.

The creaking sound was at once followed by the slow turning of the doorknob. Clare sat up with new terror in her eyes as they fixed on the gradually twisting doorknob. And as the door inched open the scream of fear which had formed in her mind froze on her paralyzed lips. Unable to move or cry out for help she watched as the door opened wide and a shadowy figure advanced into the near darkness of the bedroom. It was Belle in her flowing nightgown, her long dark tresses tumbling about her shapely shoulders, moving like a sleepwalker with her hands thrust out before her. Her face was pale and expressionless, her eyes open and staring.

The pretty maid had moved a distance across the room toward her door before Clare shook off her fear enough to get out of bed and go over to her. Belle seemed not to see or hear her as she continued slowly on her way.

Clare grasped the girl by the arm and halted her. "Belle, where have you been?" she cried.

Belle faltered and turned to stare at her with blank eyes. "I don't know," she said in a faint voice.

"You left your room to wander about like a mad creature," Clare said accusingly. "And you frightened me nearly out of my wits as you returned just now. What is your explanation?"

"I don't remember anything but the sound of the sea," Belle said in a trembling tone which indicated she was near tears.

"You must!" Clare insisted. "Are you a habitual sleepwalker?"

"Only when he was around," Belle said. "I left the house most nights then."

"You mean Barnabas?" Clare said with some alarm. For she recalled all too well that Barnabas had used his power over Belle to force her to rendezvous with him almost nightly so he could feast on her blood.

"Yes, my lady," Belle said brokenly. Now she was in tears.

Clare stared at her. "Was it Barnabas you met just now?"

"I don't know," the girl said. "I never was able to remember. All that I know is the sea was pounding. I was on the cliff and then I came back here."

"Let me light the candle," Clare said. Her fingers trembled as she found a match and the candle. Then she returned to the girl and held it up to examine her throat. The telltale red mark was there. The bite of the vampire!

Clare could only think of one answer. Barnabas must have returned during the night and influenced Belle to join him. Could the bat beating against the window have been some sort of signal for the girl? The thought sent a chill down Clare's spine.

She told the unhappy girl, "There's nothing to upset yourself about. Go back to your bed."

Belle nodded. "Yes, my lady." And she hurried on to her own room and closed the door behind her.

Clare stood indecisively with the lighted candle in her hand. Then she went to the door leading to the corridor and made her way to the stairs. Slowly she descended them with the candle held high, expecting at any moment to see Barnabas. But there was no one on the stairs or in the shadowed hallway.

She even parted the heavy drapes leading to the drawing room and looked inside, but again there was no one. Frustrated and afraid, she turned to climb the stairs again. Then she halted with a gasp.

Dr. Fontaine was standing there. He had come upon her without a sound. There was a stern look on the aquiline face and his deep-set eyes regarded her in an unfriendly fashion.

"What are you doing down here at this hour. Lady Clare?"

Clare swallowed hard. "My maid suffered a strange spell. A sort of sleepwalking. And there was a mark on her throat. The same sort of mark left by Barnabas when he used to meet her. I had an idea he might have returned."

Dr. Fontaine shook his head. "He has not come back."

"I don't understand," she said.

"You must have been mistaken about the mark," the doctor went on. "I think you are allowing your nerves to get the better of you."

"I could swear that I saw it."

The doctor frowned. "I will take a look at the girl tomorrow evening when I have finished my other work."

"It will have faded by then," Clare told him. "It takes only a few hours to vanish."

Dr. Fontaine's manner changed and he became more friendly. "I suggest you return to your bed. I'm sure you're making too much of this."

Reluctantly she let him lead her to the foot of the stairway. She hesitated to say, "Perhaps we should go back to the village and wait for the return of Barnabas there."

"Nonsense," the gray-haired doctor said. "Barnabas would never forgive me if I allowed that."

She gave the doctor a level look. "Could one of your other patients have attacked Belle?"

He shrugged. "It is unfortunate she wandered outside in her sleep. I do have several patients here who would be capable of it. Try and see that she doesn't leave her room again."

"It's very difficult," she said.

"I understand," Dr. Fontaine said. "Things will settle themselves when Barnabas returns."

She returned upstairs to her bedroom with that slight reassurance. And for the rest of the night she was mostly awake. The few restless snatches of sleep she did manage came at long intervals. Drale, the mute elderly manservant, brought their breakfast up in the morning. Belle joined her at the table in her room and she noticed that the telltale red mark had faded from the girl's throat.

"How do you feel this morning?" Clare asked her.

Belle paused over her tea. "I'm still tired and weak, my lady, in spite of my good night's sleep."

"But you didn't have a good night's sleep," Clare said. "You were out sleepwalking a good part of the night."

The girl looked baffled. "Oh, no!"

"I wakened you when you came back through this room," Clare went on. "Don't you remember?"

Belle shook her head. "I remember only falling asleep and having bad dreams."

Clare questioned her further but always got the same answer. Belle had no recollection of her sleepwalking. Discouraged by her failure to gain any information from the girl, she decided to take a walk around the grounds of the old mansion after breakfast. It was a fine day and the ancient stone building looked less forbidding in the bright sunshine.

She began to question whether she had ever seen the mark on her maid's throat. Could it have been her imagination, as the doctor had suggested? She'd been highly upset. Perhaps Belle had merely been sleepwalking with no other evil involvement. She hoped that was the case. As on the previous day there was no sign of anyone in the house or outside it. It was uncanny.

Her wandering took her beyond the bounds of the garden to a small orchard and there beneath the shade of some gnarled trees she came upon several badly weathered gravestones. The first was so badly worn she couldn't read it. But the next one she came on was in better condition. She bent to read the inscription and her eyes widened.

"Dr. Henri Fontaine, Born 1744—Died 1815." That was fifty-five years ago! And yet she had met and talked with Dr. Fontaine last night!

And then she smiled. This was undoubtedly the grave of the doctor's father, who had also been a doctor and borne the same name. She should have thought of that before. Let it be a lesson to her not to make much of every small thing she didn't immediately understand.

Moving on to the next and last gravestone she read, "Marie Fontaine, wife of Henri, Born 1780—Died 1825." This would be the doctor's mother and the inscription verified her theory of the graves being those of his parents. She left the shaded gravestones with a feeling of relief.

When she returned to the garden at the rear of the house she found Madeline Fontaine standing in the garden waiting for her. The lovely flaxen-haired woman looked even more strained than she had on their first meeting. And she still wore the same regal black velvet dress with the high neck and her single strand of pearls for decoration.

Madeline Fontaine gazed at her with a look of scorn. "Why do you stay here?"

"Because Dr. Fontaine invited me to," she said.

"You think that Barnabas will return," the doctor's wife said with almost a sneer.

She frowned. "Yes, I do. I'm waiting for him. Your husband said he would return."

"He was lying."

"I don't understand."

Madeline Fontaine took a step closer to her. "Barnabas Collins will not be back. There is nothing for him here. You have eyes! You've seen the house! What do you make of it?"

"It's badly neglected, but what has that to do with Barnabas not returning?" she demanded, becoming more upset by the minute.

Madeline laughed scornfully. "You don't recognize a house of the dead when you see it!"

"What do you mean?"

"You little fool!" the woman in black said tensely. "You've just come from the graves. Didn't you read the inscriptions?"

"Yes," Clare admitted, increasingly baffled. "Of course I did. I saw the graves of your husband's mother and father."

Madeline's thin, colorless lips twisted in a bitter smile. "You saw my husband's grave and that of his first wife!" Clare gasped.

"No!"

"Yes," Madeline said. "He is one of them. A vampire, the same as Barnabas Collins. That is why your precious Barnabas came to visit here. He was seeking a refuge, not a cure!"

Clare stood there in the bright sunshine with all her world crumbling. All the hopes she'd cherished that Barnabas might become a normal man again had been pinned on the statements of Dr. Fontaine. "He promised to cure Barnabas," she argued in dismay. "He said he would arrange it so we could be together always."

The fragile Madeline nodded grimly. "That's why he's having you stay here. Why he lied to you. He intends to have you die under his curse and become one of them!"

CHAPTER 5

Clare stood there filled with horror. "But why?"

"Because he fancies you," the woman in black said bitterly. "I married him, knowing he was a vampire and that he would feast on my blood, because he claimed eternal love for me. But now he's tired of me. And he wants you to become like him and join him in his preying on the innocent people of the island."

"That's madness!"

"Not to him," Madeline Fontaine said. "Who do you think made your servant girl walk in the moonlight last night? And who do you suppose bit into her throat and drank her blood?"

"Dr. Fontaine?"

"Who else? And you'll be the next to fall under his spell. But he has a different fate in store for you. You will become his mate. And I'll be discarded."

"I want nothing to do with your husband," Clare protested. "I've stayed here only in the hope of Barnabas coming back. If he's not returning I'll leave at once."

"The tide has risen," the woman in black told her. "You've lost your chance to escape from the island today. And tonight he plans to place his curse on you."

"I'll be safe in the village!"

"Not in the village nor anywhere else," Madeline Fontaine

predicted. "Now that he has become infatuated with you he'll pursue you. No matter where you go he'll follow you. And sooner or later he'll make you over in his pattern."

"I'll get away and find Barnabas," Clare said, terrified at the woman's prediction. "Barnabas will protect me and know how to deal with your husband."

"Barnabas has sailed for America and his home in Maine," Madeline told her. "He's far away from here on the high seas."

"Oh, no!" Clare said in dismay.

The woman's sunken eyes met hers. "There is only one way you can be saved. You must help me."

"Help you?"

"I know how to protect you from Henri, but I cannot do it alone. And I can't count on Drale to aid me. He is old and senile and dependent on my husband. But you can give me the assistance I need."

"For what?"

"To destroy Henri forever! To allow me to escape from this cursed place! When he wakes at dusk he will know that I have talked to you and told you the truth and he will kill me!"

Clare was beginning to doubt the woman's sanity. "How could he possibly know what you've said to me?"

"Even though he sleeps in his coffin, he is aware of everything that happens here," Madeline insisted, her pale face showing fear. "If we are to be saved you must help me before the day ends."

Feeling she was once again involved in a dreadful nightmare she said, "What do you want me to do?"

Madeline looked relieved. "We may as well get on with it now. Come with me."

Clare followed her, stunned. They went into the house by a rear door at the level of the cellar which she had never used. As soon as they stepped into the darkness Madeline halted to tell her, "It requires hawthorn. And I have secured what we need for just such a day. He sleeps in a corner of the wine cellar directly below the drawing room."

Madeline Fontaine moved on ahead, certain of her way even in the dank darkness, and Clare groped along behind her. As her fingers touched the slimy walls for guidance she shivered and drew back. She was still uncertain whether Madeline Fontaine had told her the truth or not, whether her hostess was a madwoman or her friend.

After they seemed to have gone an interminable way in the black depths of the cellar the doctor's wife halted again and whispered to her, "This is where I have the required items hidden."

She knelt down and seemed to be lifting the cover of a chest. A moment later she struck a light and touched the flame to a candle in a pewter holder with a handle. Now Clare could study the narrow passage hacked out of the earth and see the open chest by which Madeline knelt.

Madeline thrust the candle into her hand. "Take care of that." And next she withdrew a sharp pointed stake about two feet long and a good-sized wooden mallet from the chest. And after that a corked flask. "The holy water," she told her, handing it to her as well. "Take good care not to break the bottle. It is part of our protection." She closed the chest and rose with the stake and mallet in her hands.

"What next?" Clare asked in a low voice.

Madeline's pale face showed determination in the wavering reflection of the candle. "We go to him."

Again she led the way. When they came to the wine cellar she unlatched the wooden door and they stepped inside where high shelves held stacks of dusty bottles and great casks stood against the walls. The pungent odor of fine wine gave a bite to the air. Clare held the candle aloft to light the way for them both.

Then Madeline halted and pointed to a far corner where there were no shelves. "There," she said. And at once Clare recognized the coffin with the candles burning at either end of it. It was a replica of the sleeping place Barnabas had arranged in his London flat. She felt herself begin to tremble and had a wild desire to turn and run from the dungeon of death.

The woman in black gave her a sharp look and must have read her thoughts for she said, "Too late to back out now!"

"What are you going to do?" Clare whispered nervously.

"You'll find out," Madeline Fontaine told her. "Give me the holy water."

Clare passed it to her and waited. The doctor's wife went forward and removed the cork from the bottle, sprinkling the holy water before her and murmuring some kind of incantation. Standing close to the closed casket, she sprinkled the holy water completely around it as if she were erecting a barrier of some kind.

Now she motioned Clare to join her. Clare hesitated for only a second or two and then advanced with cautious steps. She saw that Madeline had the hawthorn stake and the mallet on the earthen floor by her feet.

Madeline's pale face was a grim mask. "Prepare yourself for a shock."

And then the woman in black turned and with some difficulty lifted up the heavy lid of the coffin to reveal a sleeping Henri Fontaine. Clare choked back an exclamation of horror with difficulty as she looked at the stem face with its sallow, corpse-like skin. And most revolting of all were the dried trickles of blood at the corners of the mouth. The doctor was indeed one of the living dead.

Madeline gave her a knowing look. Then she bent down and picked up the hawthorn stake with its sharp end. "I need your help," she whispered.

Clare mastered her loathing to move in close beside the casket. "What can I do?"

"Hold this exactly where I'm placing it," Madeline said with a strange new calm. At the same time she directed the point of the stake at approximately the location of the vampire's heart.

Clare's heart was beating wildly and she found it difficult to breathe in the dank cellar. The moldy odor of death seemed to emanate from the open coffin. She fought to keep her eyes from the pasty face befouled with blood.

"I may faint," she warned the other woman.

"Take hold of the stake," Madeline said sternly.

She did. Its point was on the chest of the vampire. Then Madeline lifted the mallet and brought it down on the stake. It sank into the body and Henri Fontaine seemed to twist in agony. Again the mallet struck hard on the stake, driving it further into the vampire. A sound like a groan came out of the casket as Madeline drove down on the stake for a third time.

Then she dropped the mallet. Taking a horrified Clare by the arm, she drew her back. Clare's eyes were riveted on the coffin where a strange and awful thing was happening. The body of Henri Fontaine seemed to curl and shrink. And as it folded in on itself its very substance seemed to disintegrate until at last there remained only a small residue of dust in the casket surrounding the stake.

"It's back to the grave for him!" Madeline Fontaine said triumphantly. "We've finished him!"

Clare still couldn't comprehend it. "His body just vanished."

"The hawthorn stake," Madeline said. "It always works. Now let's get away from here."

She was more than willing to go. And she allowed the other woman to guide her out of the cellar and up a flight of stone steps that brought them to the ground floor of the mansion again. When they reached the front hallway Madeline stopped and faced her.

"Do you want to remain here for the night or go to the inn down in the village?"

"We'll go to the inn by all means," Clare said.

"You'll have to walk. No one will come up here to get you."

"I know," Clare said. "I don't mind. Belle and I are used to long walks. And I can send the donkey cart up for our luggage tomorrow."

"Whatever you like," Madeline Fontaine said in her cool fashion. "You've earned your freedom."

"What about you?"

"I have nothing to fear here now," the woman in black said. "Perhaps I'll remain here and have the place fixed up. When the islanders learn that Henri is no longer around they may gradually lose their fear of the place and I'll be able to hire some help."

Clare frowned. "What about his patients? His hospital?"

"There never were any. No patients and no hospital. It was his story to tell strangers unwary enough to stop by here. It gave him an excuse for not showing himself in the day."

"I see," Clare said quietly. "I wish you good luck."

"Thank you. It's about time it changed for me. What about you?"

She sighed. "I shall follow Barnabas."

"After what you saw here this afternoon?" Madeline sounded unbelieving.

"It is not something I want to do. It is something I must do. Barnabas is not the kind of man your husband was. He is a kind, good person in many ways."

"I'll grant you that," the woman in black agreed grudgingly. "I found that out during the few days he was a guest here. He and that Ben. But he remains a creature of the night hours. One of the accursed!"

"Perhaps he still may be saved," Clare said.

"You will gamble your life on that? Follow him to America?"

"Yes," Clare said. "He loves his homeland and Collinwood. If there is any place he can be helped, I'd consider it the most likely."

"There is no help for vampires," Madeline Fontaine warned her. "You will soon discover that."

But Clare was no longer giving the woman in black her attention. As they'd talked in the shadowed hallway a wizened, malevolent face had appeared in the murky corridor. As Madeline finished speaking, the grotesque face vanished as quickly as it had come. Only then did Clare associate it with Drale, the mute old servant.

With a troubled glance she told Madeline, "Someone was in the corridor listening to us. I think it was Drale. He left just now."

Madeline glanced over her shoulder into the darkness, then turned to her again. "It had to be Drale," she said. "He's the only other one in the house. I don't care what he heard or knows."

"But he was very devoted to your husband," she reminded the pale woman.

"It doesn't matter. He's old and senile. I can handle him,"

Madeline Fontaine assured her.

Clare still felt uneasy. She had not liked the look of sheer hatred Drale had shown. But she said no more on the matter. She went upstairs and ordered Belle to pack their things at once.

"We're leaving this afternoon," she told the girl. "We'll take two of the small bags with us for our immediate needs and valuables. The rest of the luggage will have to wait until tomorrow. I'll try and get somebody in the village to come up here for them."

Belle looked surprised. "Then we are not waiting for Mister Barnabas?"

"He isn't returning here," Clare told her. "He's gone to America. We'll take the first crossing available and follow him there."

The girl at once busied herself packing their bags again under Clare's supervision. It was fairly late in the afternoon before they'd completed the task and were ready to leave. Clare had her cash and jewelry in the same neat leather bag in which she'd always carried them. And Belle was to bring a somewhat larger one with the clothes they would need for overnight in it.

Clare took a last glance at the room which had been hers at the old castle-like house. Its shabby, filthy condition still seemed as shocking to her as when she'd first arrived. It was truly a house of the dead. She felt Madeline was making a serious mistake in planning to remain there.

For herself, she could not escape it soon enough. She had held the stake of hawthorn which the doctor's wife had driven through his heart. Would a similar stake through the heart one day end the tempestuous career of Barnabas Collins?

Madeline Fontaine saw her and Belle through the garden to the road that wound down the rocky hillside to the peaceful village below. It was a clear day and across the island the tall old Benedictine monastery reached toward the sky. It was an awesome spectacle. And behind them was the great stone mansion, a dwarf in comparison, yet large enough and holding its own strange secrets.

The woman in black remained as aloof as always. There was a calm look on her pale face as she said, "You'll send somebody for your things tomorrow?"

"Yes," Clare said. Remembering the malevolent face of the wizened Drale again, she added, "Do be careful."

"I have no cause to worry," Madeline assured her. "I'm free at last."

They started out on the long walk down to the village, pausing to rest several places along the way. By the time they trudged into the small hotel where they'd stayed before it was close to evening.

The stout hotel owner greeted them with an amazed look. "So you have come back safely. I did not think you would."

"We managed very well," Clare told him quietly. "We would like our same rooms for the night and tomorrow we will need to get the rest of our luggage from the house on the hill."

"Oui, mam'selle," the hotel man said with grudging admiration. "You English women are even a match for ghosts or the Devil himself! With your pardon!" And he showed them upstairs.

Neither she nor Belle ate much dinner. Clare was definitely shaken by the events of the day and the dark-haired servant girl seemed even more reserved and unwilling to talk than usual. A great weariness came over Clare after dinner and so she went to bed early.

An excited shouting from the street outside the hotel woke her up. Throwing a dressing gown on over her nightdress, she left her room and went downstairs to discover what the trouble might be. The main door of the hotel was open. Loud voices were babbling out in the street.

Everyone was staring in the same direction, their eyes fastened on a great red glow in the distant sky and smoke rising high. Clare tightened her dressing gown around her and sought out the hotel owner, who was among the onlookers.

"What is it?" she asked him.

He gave her a strange look. "You do not know? It is the stone house! The house of Dr. Fontaine!"

"The house of Dr. Fontaine!" she gasped staring up at the gradually increasing red reflection of the fire in the sky. She could smell the acrid smoke.

"It is the end of an evil place," the hotel owner said in her ear. "You were lucky to escape from there when you did, mam'selle."

She gave him a worried glance. "We must do something! She is up there all alone with that old servant! I mean his wife! Surely we should try to help her."

The hotel owner shook his head. "No one will go up there tonight. I can promise you that, mam'selle."

"But she may need us!"

The hotel owner crossed himself fervently. "If she has lived there all this while with him she is beyond any help we could give her."

Clare tried to persuade him, but it was useless. So she stood there with the frightened townspeople, watching the fire come to a peak and then begin to slack down. The glow in the sky became less crimson and more a funereal mass of black smoke. Full of frustration and despair, she went back to her room and the scanty sleep that was left to her.

She couldn't erase the memory of the slim figure in black with the lovely pale face and flaxen-hair from her mind. And the following morning she persuaded the hotel owner to take her and Belle back up to the stone house in his wagon. It took a huge bribe and a good deal of pleading before he'd agree.

The sight that greeted them on reaching the mansion was a sickening one. It was completely burned out. The roof had caved in and part of the walls had come tumbling down. What was left was a shambles of crumbled walls, black empty windows and smoldering rubble. She went as close as she dared, hoping Madeline would present herself. But there was no one.

The innkeeper grew restless and finally she decided to go back. Belle had stood and stared at the ruins as if she couldn't believe what she saw. Now they all got in the wagon for the ride back to the village.

Clare touched the arm of the hotel owner. "On the way I'd like to stop by that distant clump of trees. There are several graves there."

The stout man gave her a grim look. He murmured something under his breath but in a louder voice said, "Oui, mam'selle."

So she was able to descend from the wagon and spend a last few minutes by the grave of Henri Fontaine. What struck her at once was the huge crevice which had appeared and ran almost the length of the grave, a dry crack in the earth. And on the adjoining grave of his wife, Marie, there was an almost identical crevice in the grassy mound. Neither of them had been there when she'd visited the graves yesterday.

She was still standing there staring at the graves when the hotel owner joined her. He crossed himself again before he spoke. Then he said, "You see the openings in the graves. They have used them to return to their resting places. Maybe the island is rid of their curse at last!"

Clare looked at him in amazement. "You don't really believe that?"

"It is often so," he assured her. "The vampires use such means to rise from the grave and return to it again."

She silently followed him back to the wagon where Belle was waiting for them. Yet the man's words had started her thinking all sorts of wild things, things she would ordinarily have refused to countenance. And as the carriage wheels creaked along the dusty road she wondered if he might be right. And another shocking possibility crossed her mind.

Had she really known a Madeline Fontaine or had the

woman in black also been a vampire? Had the lovely pale face and flaxen hair belonged to Marie, whose grave lay next to her husband's? And had a jealous Marie used her to eliminate the man ready to discard her love? It was a far-out possibility. Just as it was possible that Drale was one of them as well, who had avenged his master by setting fire to the castle-like mansion and destroying Marie along with himself. She'd never be sure about it. The episode of Mont St. Michel would always haunt her.

So when the tide allowed the following day they rode back to the mainland. From there they journeyed to Paris where Clare purchased a fresh wardrobe for both herself and Belle. The servant girl lost some of her forlorn reserve in the excitement of the shopping spree. It was a happy time for both of them.

Clare had questioned Belle again about the events of that night on the island, knowing full well that she'd met Henri Fontaine on the cliffs and that he'd satiated himself with her blood. But the girl honestly seemed to have no recollection of the dark happenings. And since she had now gotten over the effects on her health of the loss of blood, Clare decided there would be no good purpose served in discussing it further. So she dropped the subject completely.

They next took the boat train back from Calais to Dover. But they did not return to London. Clare was loath to do this because she was afraid her father might find a way to end her travelings. Also she had heard there were a number of ships making passage from Liverpool to Boston. And since she knew Boston to be close to Maine and the town of Collinsport where Barnabas had been born, she decided to make Liverpool her destination.

The train journey there was a tiring one and they spent several days in the modest lodgings Clare had secured for them before venturing out into the city. Her first call was on a famous banking house where she arranged to draw some funds from her London account and also have a good amount of cash transferred to a bank in Boston for her use in America.

The full-bearded, pompous man who was manager of the banking firm seemed to doubt her wisdom in going to the New World. He frowned across his desk at her. "I dislike the idea of two young women venturing to visit America alone," he said. "It is a wild country full of Indians and outlaws. And the great cities along the coast are seething with ruffians, the cast-offs of every country in Europe."

"I have heard rather different accounts of the country," Clare said with an air of defiance. "And I plan to visit friends in Maine. So there is no need to worry."

The big man raised his heavy black eyebrows. "As you

say, Lady Duncan. I take it your father is aware of your plans and approves?"

"My father is very much occupied with his duties in the House and his other affairs," Clare said airily. "As I am busy with mine. You will see that the transfer of cash is properly made?"

The man with the full black beard nodded. "You may depend on that. I assume you have arranged for your passage?"

Clare was wary about giving him any more details of her plans. From the beginning she had found his attitude suspicious. She had not yet settled on a ship, but she decided it would be wiser not to confide this fact in him.

"My friend in America made the arrangements from that end," she said in her assured way as she rose to leave the office. Her assurance was a good deal of a bluff but the banker could not possibly know this.

He saw her to the door with great dignity. "You understand it will take a month or more to complete the credit to the bank in Boston," he warned her as she was leaving.

"Yes," she said. "But I'm certain you will give the matter your best attention."

"You need not fear on that score, my lady." He bowed her out onto the street.

As soon as she was alone and walking toward the district where the shipping offices were she began to worry. The banker had shown too much concern about her project and made too many inquiries about her father. He might get in touch with Lord Duncan.

The thought continued to trouble her as she made the rounds of the various shipping offices; she would book the earliest possible passage across the Atlantic. Desperately worried about Barnabas Collins and his safety, she felt that the sooner she saw him again the happier she would be.

A young man behind the counter of the Liverpool and London Steamship Company proved to have the ideal answer to her problem. "We can book you passage on our next sailing, miss," he assured her with a smile. "It leaves in four days."

Clare sighed. "Have you nothing before? I wish to get to Boston as soon as possible."

"This is the quickest and best way," the young man promised her with a smile. "The Morning Star is a speedy ship and you should reach there in less than a fortnight if the weather holds."

She gave him a delighted look. "That's wonderful!" The idea of being in America in such a short time filled her with hope again. Before a month passed she would surely be at Collinwood with Barnabas. She quickly booked passages for herself and Belle, giving false names in both instances.

The clerk glanced at the form she had completed. "I'm positive you'll be pleased with the vessel," he said. "You will board the evening before she is due to sail."

"Is the Morning Star a steamboat with a sidewheel?" she wanted to know. She had heard of the marvelous speed and comfort of the great sidewheelers.

The clerk shook his head and said proudly, "No, miss. She's a screw propeller, the latest type. They do claim that within a few years ships with screw propellers will be crossing the Atlantic in a week!"

Clare left the steamship office marveling at the great new age she lived in and wondering what startling changes it would make in the pattern of things.

She hurried back to their lodgings and told Belle the good news. The pretty dark-haired girl was greatly excited at the prospect of crossing the ocean. Clare also mentioned her interview at the bank and her suspicions that the manager might attempt to contact her father. "So we will remain close to our rooms until we are ready to leave," she told the maid.

They did, although the days seemed interminably long. But at last the evening before the sailing arrived and Clare asked her landlady to have a cab come for them to take them to the docks.

While they were waiting for the cab they heard a carriage draw up before the house, followed by a loud knocking on the front door. Clare, who was sitting in her room with Belle, their luggage waiting on the floor, gave the maid an apprehensive glance and stepped quickly to the door to listen.

From below she heard a too-familiar voice boom out, "I'm Lord Augustus Duncan. I understand my daughter and her maid are living here in this house. And I demand to see them at once!"

CHAPTER 6

Clare waited to hear no more. She ran back to the room, seized a startled Belle by the hand and dragged her out of the room and down the hall to a closet where the landlady kept mops and brooms and other cleaning supplies. It was small, black and stuffy, but she felt it would make the ideal hiding place if they were both able to squeeze into it.

She pushed Belle ahead into the closet without giving her a chance to utter a question or complaint and then joined her and somehow managed to close the door on them. Pressed tightly against the other girl, she knew they wouldn't be able to stay in there long without being overcome from the foul air. But she hoped they could manage to stay until her father had gone.

There was a rumble of voices and steps on the stairs. The landlady's high-pitched complaining mingled with her father's sonorous insistence that he inspect the room. Then they were in the hall and dangerously close to the closet. Clare scarcely dared breathe and prayed that Belle would make no sound. Her father and the landlady advanced into the room and remained there for a few minutes.

After that the voices became louder as they emerged from the room. Next there was the retreat down the stairs again with the sound of the talk gradually fading. Several minutes later the front door opened and slammed closed and Clare felt it reasonable to assume that her father had gone.

Cautiously she left the closet and nodded to Belle to follow. "It's probably all right now," she whispered to the maid. "I think my father has left."

"What shall we do, miss?" Belle said in a troubled voice.

"Carry on with our plans," she told her. "My father can't possibly know the ship we're taking. We'll leave and get aboard before he returns."

Clare went downstairs and found the elderly landlady in a state of nerves. The old woman had a nervous twitch and it was worse than ever at the moment.

She wrung her hands on seeing Clare and said, "Your father has just been here and caused a dreadful commotion! I had no idea you were a titled lady, miss. Your father is a very unforgiving man and he seemed to have the idea I knew who you were from the start."

"Don't worry about him," she consoled the old woman. "His threats are much worse than his actions. Where did he go?"

"Off to see some banker friend," the landlady said despairingly, the twitch in her eye very noticeable. "But he warned he would be back and he would expect to see you."

"Let him expect!" Clare said indignantly. "We're leaving."

"But he'll want me to tell him where you've gone," the old woman lamented.

"You can't tell him if you don't know," Clare reminded her. "And you don't know."

With that she went upstairs and told Belle they were leaving at once. Then she went outside and walked to the corner where she waited until the first empty hansom cab came by and hailed it. Within a few minutes they were packed and on their way to the docks.

There was a slight fog. Although nothing compared to the ones in London, it was still sufficient to wreathe the Liverpool docks in a ghostly mist. Although it was growing dark they were still at work loading the Morning Star. Torches had been set up along the work area and men toiled, sweated and cursed over great cases being transferred to the vessel. All was bustle and confusion. The cab was able to drive right out on the dock and the driver waited until she had secured the attention of the ship's officer who was supervising the loading. On discovering she was a passenger, he dispatched a man to show them aboard and help them with their luggage.

The sailor was respectful and helpful. He saw their luggage safely on deck and then took them down to their stateroom, which was not too far below. It was a stateroom for four and already there were two spinster sisters from Philadelphia in it. They at once told Clare they were returning from a year long visit to the continent. They were in their sixties, friendly, with thin gray hair and rather pointed features. Their chief worry was that they would be seasick.

Clare acknowledged their remarks pleasantly, and introduced Belle as her friend, rather than her maid. It was part of her plan for concealing who she was in case her father made a round of the docks seeking her. Nervously they waited for the great vessel to cast off. As it turned out she was asleep when it did. The gentle motion of the waves and the pounding of the steam engine driving the ship woke her up.

It was still foggy when she and Belle went out on deck. Land was out of sight because of the fog. But Clare was not in a mood to mind the weather. She was too happy to be on her way.

Turning to Belle, who was leaning against the rail with her, she said, "Think of it, Belle! It's only a question of two weeks or more before I see Barnabas Collins again."

The dark-haired girl showed concern. "How can you be sure he's gone to America and Collinwood?"

"Because that woman on Mont St. Michel told me so and I'm sure she wasn't lying," Clare said. "And it's the most likely thing he would have done."

Their first day aboard the big vessel was an interesting one. The sea was calm and they appeared to be making good progress despite the slight mist that remained to reduce visibility. The public rooms were large and luxuriously furnished and the food appeared to be very good. Tea was served in the late afternoon, much to the pleasure of the spinster sisters from Philadelphia. And all four of them received invitations to dine with the captain at his table on the first evening of the crossing.

Lydia Southbridge, the elder of the sisters, confided to Clare, "We are being honored because we are occupying the most expensive stateroom. But we are surely entitled to the distinction since Prudence and I come from one of Philadelphia's fine families. And I'm sure you have good breeding. It shows, my dear. And your little dark-haired friend is nice, although so quiet."

Clare quickly alibied for the pretty Belle. "She has not been away from her parents before," she said. "But her father is a very successful man in the import trade. She is visiting friends of his in America."

"How nice!" Lydia said with an approving smile on her pinched face.

Dressing for the dinner party was such fun that Clare forgot for a time the shadow that was still over her. Even the terrible events she had experienced before leaving Europe were blotted from her mind by the joyful excitement of the occasion. The two spinsters provided a good deal of amusement for both her and Belle. Like young women on a first date, Lydia and Prudence worried over several choices of dress and jewels before settling on prim black highlighted with a discreet locket for each woman.

The captain proved to be a genial man in his early fifties, with mutton-chop whiskers. He was quite bald. He seated them at his table with a fluttery Lydia on his right. Clare saw that there were still two vacant chairs at the table but a few minutes later a man and a woman came forward to fill them. The captain rose to greet the newcomers and introduce them.

"This is Mr. Josef Palladino the celebrated medium and his wife and assistant, the charming Mrs. Palladino."

The introduction caused a general stir around the table. The Palladinos were well dressed and extremely good looking. They sat down with a great deal of dignity. Studying them, Clare was certain they were not ordinary people. The little she'd heard about spiritualism had given her the impression most of the practitioners were charlatans. She did not think this was likely in the case of the Palladinos.

The captain filled in a lull at the table by saying, "Mr. Palladino and his wife are going to tour the United States giving a series of seances."

Lydia's pinched face brightened. "How interesting!" she chirped. "Do you specialize in table-tapping, or perhaps you and your lovely wife levitate? I once saw a medium float out the door of a room and in the window."

Josef Palladino looked displeased. "My wife and I do not indulge in such gymnastics," he said with a slight foreign accent. "We prefer to try and penetrate the veil of the spirit world and conduct conversations with the dead."

The younger sister, Prudence, gasped at this. "You can really summon up the dead, Mr. Palladino?"

The man with the burning eyes nodded. "Yes, madam." And he said it with such finality it sent a chill through Clare. And she noticed it brought another lull in the conversation at the table.

The captain came to the rescue again. Tugging at a sandy mutton-chop whisker he said, "Jolly good trick if you can manage it. No question about that."

Clare felt she should contribute something to the table talk. With a flattering smile she suggested, "Perhaps you will give us a sample of your powers before the voyage is over, Mr. Palladino."

"I should like to do that if the opportunity presents itself," he replied gravely.

"By all means," the captain said heartily. "Positive the passengers would enjoy it. Anything to dispel the monotony of the crossing."

That fortunately ended the discussion of seances. The talk moved on to other things, with the captain dwelling on his experiences in the Pacific—especially his numerous narrow escapes from islands peopled entirely by bloodthirsty natives. Clare felt he might be exaggerating more than a little but it made good listening. The Southbridge sisters were thrilled; apparently they had donated heavily to the missionary field.

To all intents the voyage was going to be a placid and interesting one. Several days and nights went by with the weather staying good and the seas remaining relatively calm for the Atlantic. Still both the Southbridge sisters spent some time in their bunks until their queasy stomachs adjusted to the roll of the Morning Star.

Embarrassed at playing the role of Clare's friend, Belle became even more silent than ever. And she absented herself from the stateroom and the spinsters' questionings whenever she could. Clare sympathized with the pretty maid and regretted that she'd placed her in the awkward position. But it had seemed the wise thing to do when she'd booked their passages.

Clare often took walks on the upper deck alone. And one night when she was taking a stroll to enjoy the star filled sky that dipped to the rolling ocean in every direction, she was startled by someone coming up behind her. Turning quickly, she recognized the medium, Josef Palladino.

He smiled. "You will forgive me. But we have been dinner companions and I felt you would not mind my joining you. My wife does not like traveling by water and is spending most of the time in our stateroom."

She returned his smile. "That is a pity," she said. "It is so lovely out here tonight."

His burning amber eyes raised to scan the starry night. "You are right," he agreed quietly. "It is the sort of night one feels close to the universe."

"That would have a special meaning for you," she said.

"And for you as well, if I'm not mistaken," he said, studying her earnestly. "From the first meeting with you I have felt certain emanations that link you with the spirit world."

Clare at once knew a sense of alarm. Had her love for Barnabas Collins left its mark on her so clearly? Did the fact that she had given her heart to a man who was not truly dead, but one of the living dead, set her apart from others?

She felt she should discourage the medium's investigation of her private affairs. She was afraid he would learn too much. "You're quite wrong about that," she said. "I'm not at all psychic."

Josef Palladino's handsome face showed skepticism. "You may wish to fool me, but you cannot. I am sensitive to these things. There is some affinity between you and the dead. What it is I don't know, but it is there."

"You're trying to frighten me, Mr. Palladino," she said in a thin voice.

"It could also be that I am trying to warn you."

"I'm sure you're in error this time, she said. "But then,I suppose you do occasionally make mistakes."

He shrugged. "I could have made an error in mentioning this to you. I am sorry. Accept my apologies."

"Don't worry about it," she said with an attempt at lightness. "Let us continue our stroll and enjoy the stars." Arid they did. No more was said of spirits. The medium escorted her to the door of her stateroom and bid her goodnight. Yet he had upset her, and when she entered the shadowed stateroom and discovered the others deep in slumber, with Lydia, the elder of the sisters, snoring loudly, she found herself with no desire for sleep.

For a long time she lay awake with a frown on her pretty face. She was thinking of Barnabas and what would happen when they met. Now that the time for the meeting drew near she began to worry that he might resent her following him. He might turn his back on her. Or there might be no way to rescue him from his accursed state.

These tormenting thoughts led to the nightmare-filled sleep that followed. In her dreams she was back on the island of Mont St. Michel, a captive of the sinister Dr. Fontaine. Deep in the dungeon-like cellar of the old house she was a prisoner in a cage with wooden bars closely set together. She was gripping the bars and screaming for help when the hateful old doctor came along the corridor toward her.

His hairy, claw-like hands unlocked the door of her cage. As she tried to escape her prison he blocked the way with a tiendish expression on his aquiline face. The powerful hands gripped her roughly and she was repelled by the fetid, bloody stench of his breath in her face.

"Now you become one of us," he said with a leering smile as he bared his prominent white fangs of teeth.

"No!" she screamed.

But it was useless to scream or struggle. She was helpless in his powerful grasp. And so he sank his teeth deep in her throat, tearing at her throat, spilling her blood.

"No!" she screamed again but in a weaker voice as her

strength drained.

And then she was awake sitting up in her bunk and a distraught Lydia Southbridge in bonnet and nightgown was standing by her. "Whatever is wrong?" the spinster quavered.

"I'm sorry," she apologized, conscious of the cold clammy sweat that covered her body.

"Such screams! You must have had a dreadful nightmare!"

"I did," Clare said wearily. "I'm sorry I woke you."

"And what about your friend, Belle?" the spinster wanted to know. "She's not in her bunk. She's gone!"

"She can't be!" Clare protested, as alarmed in reality as she had been in her nightmare.

The spinster stood back and pointed to the upper bunk. "It's empty."

Clare was on her feet now and staring up at the empty bunk. She quickly threw a coat over her nightgown and hurried from the cabin.

There was only the pound of the engine together with the wash of the sea to break the midnight silence as the great vessel moved forward in the darkness. Clare held the coat tight around her to protect herself from the chill night air. Brushing back the loose hair the slight breeze wafted over her eyes, she strained to catch some glimpse of the missing Belle.

She'd gone almost the length of the lower deck and was going to try the other side of the ship when she glanced up and saw the girl on the deck above. Belle was clad only in her light nightdress and walking as if in a daze. There was no question that she was sleepwalking again.

Clare hurried to the upper deck and caught up with the unfortunate girl. Grasping her by the arm she shook her and cried, "Belle, what are you doing out here?"

The dark-haired girl stared at her with incredulous eyes. "Where am I?" She looked around dazedly.

"Alone on this upper deck and sleepwalking," Clare reprimanded her. "You might have fallen over the side and been lost without anyone knowing about it." She put her arm around the girl and started to lead her back.

Belle began to sob. "I had a dream! A bad dream!"

"What kind of dream?"

"I saw him!" the girl sobbed.

"Who?"

"That awful Dr. Fontaine! It was the same sort of dream I had the night I wandered to the cliff."

Terror rose chokingly in her throat again. She could make no reply for a moment. Automatically she glanced at the trembling girl's neck to see if the familiar mark of the vampire was there. But she could see nothing in the darkness of the deck.

"Come along," she finally managed in a soothing voice. "We must get you back in bed before you catch your death of cold."

She finally got Belle down to the stateroom and in her bunk. Then she had to placate the two Southbridge sisters, who were both awake. At last she stretched out in her own bunk and shut her eyes from sheer exhaustion.

Of course she could not sleep. And with the need to take care of the others removed her own fears came sweeping back once more. There had to be something awry! There was too much coincidence to it all! Josef Palladino, the medium, had first told her that he sensed a link with the spirit world in her. Then she had suffered that horrible dream in which Henri Fontaine had tried to turn her into a vampire. And Belle had also had a dream with the sinister doctor in it that had sent her into one of her sleepwalking spells.

What did it all add up to? The possible answer frightened her more than anything that had gone before. For she was beginning to believe that somehow from beyond the grave the evil Dr. Fontaine was avenging himself on her, still exerting an influence over her and over Belle. If that was the case they were both in awful danger.

The following afternoon she had what seemed a definite confirmation of her suspicions. She was out on the deck alone, since a light blow had come up and it was too rough for most of the others. As the big vessel pounded its way through the giant waves and dipped at every meeting with them, she leaned by the rail to watch the foam-capped crests. She was relaxed and enjoying this gentle sampling of the fury the sea could hurl against them in an angrier mood when a thoroughly terrifying thing happened.

It was as if some whirlwind had abruptly caught her in its toils and lifted her and projected her over the railing. She screamed and fought to grasp the rail, feeling herself going over into the turmoil of the sea below. Just as it seemed certain she was lost she felt strong hands grasp her and pull her back.

The shadowed, handsome face of Josef Palladino stared at her in utter disbelief as he continued to hold her by the shoulders. "Why did you attempt to leap overboard?"

"I didn't!" she said. "Something caught hold of me and lifted me!"

His amber eyes showed disbelief. "I was not far away. I saw you. You deliberately tried to jump over."

She shook her head. "You're wrong. It was an illusion."

"You'd be in the water now if I hadn't caught you," was his

answer. And he let her go.

Clare touched a hand to her temple forlornly. "I don't understand. I just don't understand!"

"Perhaps now you will believe there are forces working against you of which you have no knowledge," the medium suggested.

She gave him a frightened glance. "I don't want to believe that!"

"I've understood that from the beginning," the handsome medium said. "Tonight you will have a chance to discover the truth. The captain has asked me to conduct a seance for the passengers. With your permission I should like to have you serve as one of my subjects."

Her first impulse was to refuse. And then she thought better of it. If evil spirits were trying to destroy her she'd be wise to discover all she could about them.

She said, "Very well. If you like."

"I want to help you," he said sincerely. "And in the meantime I suggest you be extra careful."

Clare hardly needed the good advice the medium had offered her. She was convinced that something of the sinister Dr. Fontaine had survived and was trying to end her existence as she had ended his. He had not forgiven her for the stake she'd helped drive through his heart. And he was also trying to wreak his vengeance on the unfortunate Belle.

The seance was scheduled in the passengers' dining room at nine o'clock. The Southbridge sisters were delighted; they had often attended spiritualistic meetings and were intent on getting some communication from their parents. Clare found it hard to enter into their enthusiasm for the affair, which she was actually dreading. And she had a difficult time getting Belle to agree to go at all.

"I'm afraid," the dark-haired girl said despairingly.

"You'll be surrounded by other people," Clare consoled her. "There's nothing to fear." But she didn't feel all that sure about it herself.

The dining room was in almost complete darkness. And the passengers attending the seance seemed to be affected by the somber mood Josef Palladino was deliberately establishing. On a small raised platform was a square enclosure with white cloth sides in which his wife was already seated. The cloth at the front which served as a door was hung aside so she could be plainly seen.

Clare, Belle and the two spinsters took seats together down front. When the last of the passengers had found chairs Josef Palladino stood on the platform with his wife.

"In a few minutes," he said, "this room will be plunged in complete darkness. I will then try to contact some of the departed spirits close to those of you gathered here. My wife will act as the medium. And I beg of you not to move or cry out when the seance is in progress. Otherwise the spirits will be frightened off, the link broken."

Belle turned to give her a worried look and Clare mouthed silently, "It will be allright."

Josef Palladino addressed his audience, "We must strive for vibrations of harmony, make our minds receptive to the mystery about to be revealed to us." He stepped down from the stage and touched Clare's shoulder. "I should like to use this young woman for my initial test." He gave her a reassuring glance.

Then he stepped back on the stage and asked that the remaining lights be doused. In the pitch blackness that followed he closed the white flap at the front of the tentlike affair in which his wife was sitting.

"Now," he said in a hollow voice, "we shall try to contact the spirit close to the young woman I designated." His wife began a kind of chant like some odd hymn . . . but yet it was not a hymn. It went on for what seemed a very long time and Clare began to get terribly uneasy.

Suddenly the chanting ended and the medium's wife gave a hoarse scream. "You killed me!" the words came from her in a different voice, a voice that sent an icy dagger through Clare. It resembled a voice she had recently known—the voice of Dr. Henri Fontaine.

And now over the stage and directly in front of her a nebulous glow was showing itself, a phosphorescent fog. A circle of glowing fog that began to take shape as something else. A man's head. The head of the sinister Dr. Fontaine! Clare gasped and Belle screamed aloud as the evil face smiled at them. It was a smile of warning.

From the enclosure in which the medium's wife sat there came a kind of moaning gibberish and then a hoarse cry in a different voice, "My power! My power over his!" As the words issued from the lips of the woman in the enclosure a change took place in the glowing face of Henri Fontaine. His features faded very gradually and began to be replaced by others. The change took place in a matter of seconds until a new face showed in the glowing circle of fog. The gaunt, handsome face of Barnabas Collins. Belle clutched Clare's arm. "It's Mister Barnabas," she moaned in fear.

"Be calm!" Clare begged in a whisper, though by this time she was upset badly enough herself.

Barnabas stared at her with infinite sadness on his familiar features. She felt that if she took a step or two toward the stage she could actually touch the weary face. But then as she watched he also faded and only the glowing circle of fog was left.

"I will move on to another subject," Josef Palladino said from the darkness. And he did.

The evening progressed as he made contacts for others in the audience. But while there were voices issuing from the mouth of the medium's wife there was no repetition of the glowing circle with the faces in it. Clare's head was throbbing so that she felt ill and she paid little attention.

At last it ended and the gas lamps were lighted again. As the seance broke up Lydia Southbridge rose from her chair with a sniff. "There wasn't much but fakery to it that I could see," she said. "All that gibberish from the woman and that glow they had on the stage at the beginning. I expect he produced it by burning some kind of incense."

Clare glanced at her in disbelief. "Didn't you see the faces?"

"What faces?" the spinster asked sharply.

"It wasn't important," Clare said quickly and gave Belle a warning glance. For she suddenly realized that she and Belle were the only ones in all the gathering who had seen the faces of Dr. Fontaine and Barnabas Collins. They were the only ones who had been meant to see them.

As she and Belle headed for the exit Josef Palladino strode toward them. He halted in front of her and fixed his burning amber eyes on her. "You know what happened during the seance tonight?"

She nodded. "I saw the faces."

"More than the faces," he assured her solemnly. "There was a struggle between an evil force and a protective one. The force which has been bent on destroying you was conquered. You need fear it no longer. Your Barnabas Collins was the victor."

"How do you know all this?" she asked incredulously.

"My wife was the medium tonight," he said. "She told me of the struggle. And she told me to warn you. She sees no happiness ahead for you and this Barbabas. It is all darkness!"

CHAPTER 7

Clare was going to remember the warning many times in the months ahead. But at that moment she bitterly resented the medium's words and his intrusion into her affairs.

She answered him coldly, "Thank you, Mr. Palladino. But I'm certain you and your wife are somehow confused regarding my future."

"I doubt that," the swarthy man said impassively.

"I appreciate your concern," she said. "But my friend and I are both very tired. So if you will excuse us we'll return to our stateroom."

The medium bowed stiffly as they left him. Clare did not actually try to avoid Palladino for the balance of the voyage, but she made no attempt to engage in a personal conversation with him. He had upset her too much.

The Morning Star entered Boston Harbor on a fine morning in August. She and Belle said good-bye to the sisters from Philadelphia and when they left the ship, found overnight accommodation at the famous Parker House just a short distance from Boston Common. Clare discussed getting to Maine and Collinwood with the desk clerk at the hotel and discovered there was a train leaving for Bangor the next morning.

"It leaves at seven," the mustached clerk behind the desk

told her. "And it arrives in Bangor in the early evening. There is a connecting branch line which passes through the town of Collinsport. It's known as the Shore Line. You will have to make a transfer to it. I'm afraid it will mean arriving in town after dark. Will you have someone to meet you?"

"Not really," she said. "But no doubt I can manage some sort of transportation at the railway station."

The clerk pursed his lips. "Perhaps. You can't count on it late in the evening in a small town. But the railway agent might be able to help you."

"We'll hope so," Clare told him with a smile. "I'll take the Bangor train in the morning."

Clare's anticipation grew as her rendezvous with Barnabas Collins at Collinwood drew nearer. She was full of hopes that she'd be able to help him in some way and the horror that she'd witnessed in London that night would be wiped from her mind forever. Apprehensive that he might resent her following him, she thought of ways to explain her motives so he would understand.

Belle was silent as usual, showing strain as the hour for their meeting Barnabas again came close. Clare worried a little about her and promised herself she would let Barnabas understand he was to victimize the maid no more. It would be the first step on his road to normalcy. At least that was how she saw it.

The train journey to Bangor proved rewarding as far as the scenery was concerned. But the ride was rough and the seats in the carriages not too comfortable. The dining car offered good plain food but no more. And they were thoroughly weary of the trip by the time they arrived at the busy station of the large Maine city.

The branch-line train looked small and poor compared to the one they'd just left. It carried only two baggage cars along with two passenger coaches. Transferring to it meant only a short walk across to another track where the smaller engine was already under steam.

Clare and Belle settled themselves on one of the plain wooden seats in the gas-lit railway carriage. Clare gave the maid a resigned smile. "We can count ourselves lucky we have not more than a few hours to spend on this line."

Since the train made numerous stops, they seemed to be halted at tiny stations longer than they were traveling. Night had fallen and there was nothing to see from the carriage windows. Some of the men were smoking and heavy clouds of strong tobacco smoke spiraled down the car's length. The conductor came and punched their tickets and told them they would arrive in Collinsport at ten-fifteen.

It was closer to ten-thirty when Clare was assisted down on the platform of the small station with Belle following timidly after her. The trainman, a big burly man with a strong Maine accent, was anxious to be helpful.

"Luggage will be waitin' up front by the baggage car, miss," he said tipping his cap. "Reckon you're the only passengers gettin' off here."

And they were. By the time they had reached their several bags and suitcases, the ancient engine of the train was asthmatically gathering steam to be on its way. The station agent, a doleful, wizened man in official cap, vest and shirt sleeves with a clip of shipping papers under his arm, gave them a bleak greeting.

"Where you two ladies aimin' to go?" he wanted to know. "You expected at the hotel?"

"No," Clare said. "We have come to visit a friend. A Mr. Barnabas Collins. I imagine he is living with his family at Collinwood."

The little man frowned. "Him! The one that's come here from England?"

"Yes," Clare said, noting the distaste in the agent's voice as he mentioned England.

"He's not living at Collinwood," the agent informed her. "He's rented Stormcliff. That's a stone house on the Collins property. Him and that queer servant of his are down there. So you're friends of his?" He said it with a hint of disapproval.

"Yes, I met Mr. Collins in London," Clare said. "How can we get to this Stormcliff?"

"You'll need a carriage," the station agent said. "And there ain't none here."

"I can see that."

"Won't be, neither. Hardly anyone ever arrives on the night train so Jeb never comes down to meet it. He's the livery stable man."

"Have you any suggestions?" Clare asked.

The agent rubbed his bony chin doubtfully. "I got a wagon. And I'll be leavin' soon as I lock up. But it means going a distance out of my way."

"We'll be glad to pay you," Clare told him.

He looked a lot less reluctant. "Then I reckon we can take care of the problem," he said. "Mind you, it ain't any fancy wagon. You and your friend will have to sit on the driver's seat with me."

"As long as you've room for our luggage in the rear."

"Lot's of room," the little man said. He glanced up at a

dark sky without stars. "Been threatenin' a thunderstorm, but it ain't sprung up yet. Reckon it won't before I get you two to where you're goin.'"

He left them in the darkness to go lock up and fetch his wagon. Clare was feeling a little nervous. The country night was frighteningly quiet now that the train had gone. And the knowledge that she was about to see Barnabas soon again also made her edgy. Turning to Belle, she said, "Our long journey will soon be at an end."

The maid asked, "But will Mr. Barnabas take us as guests? He doesn't know we are coming." There was an uneasy note in her voice.

Clare tried to sound an assurance she didn't feel. "Of course, he will. He is bound to have more room for us than if he were himself a guest at Collinwood."

The creak of wagon wheels and the sight of the lantern hanging from the frame wagon alerted them to the approach of the station agent. With an agility not to be expected in one of his frail frame and age he transferred the bags to the rear of the rig and helped them up onto the wagon seat with Belle in the middle. When the swayback mare started off with them Clare had to grip the seat firmly to steady herself against the rough ride.

To make conversation, she asked, "How does there happen to be two large houses on the estate?"

"Stormcliff was built about twenty years ago by Peter Collins for his bride. She weren't in the house for more than a few months when she fell off a horse she was ridin' and broke her neck. Happened right by the stables. They do say Peter Collins came out and when he saw what had happened he got a gun and shot the horse dead. He acted as if he was goin' out of his mind for a while. Then he shut up the house, sold his share in the family business and left Collinsport."

"Where did he go?" Clare asked.

"Nobody seems to have ever heard," the agent said. "One of the other Collins brothers lived in the house for awhile. But his wife didn't like it and so they went back to Collinwood. Then an uncle came and stayed there until he died. He was killed in an accident at the fish packing factory."

"It doesn't sound like a lucky house," she said.

"Now that's a fact," the agent agreed as they drove along slowly through the darkness. "And I guess it's just as well you know about it. House has been closed up tight until this Barnabas Collins comes along. Now he and his servant are living there. People around here don't know what to make of them."

"Why is that?"

"They act so odd," the agent said. "That Ben won't talk to anyone. He comes into town to buy provisions and hardly has two words to say. And he sure don't encourage visitors to the place. As for that Barnabas Collins himself, the only time anybody sees him is after dark. He walks around in that cape and carrying a cane like a real moneyed English gent. Which is what he is, I suppose. Guess a lot of the town girls have their eyes on him. He's good lookin' in a kind of funny way."

"I know what you mean," she said.

The agent gave her a sharp glance. "What makes you two think you'll be welcome? You relatives or something?"

"Just friends."

"Wouldn't surprise me if you were relatives," he went on. "The Collins family have got kinfolks all over. Richest family in Collinsport."

"Barnabas told me that," she said.

"You two girls have a Limey accent," the station agent said. "You both from England?"

"Yes. This is our first visit to America."

"Well, this here town is part of it," the old man said sagely. "You want to watch your step goin' out at night, though. There's been some peculiar things happening here lately."

"Really?" Clare asked in a strained voice.

"You betcha," the station agent said laconically. "Young girl was found strangled in a field behind the bar in town. She weren't no better than she should be, but folks didn't like what happened. Specially since three or four other girls claim they've had close calls from being attacked by some mystery man."

Clare decided it might well be Barnabas rampant in his thirst for blood. She hoped he hadn't been involved in the murder which had been mentioned, and yet she knew there was a real danger he might be guilty of it.

They took a side road that seemed little more than a lane. Along the way the driver told them, "If there's to be any lights you'll see them from Stormcliff. The family in the big house, Collinwood, are all away for a little. Believe they went to New York City. So there are only the servants there now and they live downstairs in the rear. You wouldn't see the lights from this road."

Clare was surprised to learn that the Collins family were not at home. She said, "Then Barnabas is temporarily the only Collins left on the estate."

"That's so, miss," the driver said.

They drove on along the road until in the distance a massive stone house stood framed against the dark sky. A single strong lantern hung above its entrance door and its glow threw the fine mansion into highlight. But there seemed to be no lights inside.

"There's Stormcliff," the station agent said grimly.

"It's larger than I expected," she said.

"The Collins family never do things in a small way," the old man said. "But they don't seem to have much luck. Least that's what folks around here always say."

Clare couldn't help wondering if the legend of ill luck hadn't first arisen with the curse that Barnabas bore, the curse which had begun with Angelique.

They were close to the imposing stone house now and the agent brought the wagon to a halt. He eyed the lantern hanging over the door and the dark windows grimly.

"Ought to be someone home," he said. "Can't tell for sure since there don't seem to be any lights inside."

"Let us try anyway," Clare suggested.

The agent helped her and Belle down from the wagon. All three of them converged on the front door. The agent took the initiative and banged his bony fist on the stout oaken door. Then they waited.

From overhead there was a rumble of thunder and after a brief flash of lightning. This was followed by an ominous quiet again. The agent glanced up at the sky with a practiced eye. "Expect that storm will break mighty soon. Chances are I'll get caught in it before I manage the drive home."

"I'm sorry," Clare said.

"You'll be lucky if you aren't in it, too," the old man replied. "I don't think we're going to have any luck here." And he pounded on the door again.

Belle spoke up. "Look! There's a light in the hallway now!"

"Then there is somebody here after all," Clare said with relief.

The oaken door swung open to reveal Ben standing there with a lamp in his right hand. The stooped old servant showed uneasiness and surprise at seeing them gathered on the steps. "Yes?" he asked in his reedy voice.

"You got some visitors," the station agent informed him. "And I have their luggage here."

Seeing that Ben still did not recognize her, Clare came a step closer and drew back the hood of the cape she was wearing so he could fully see her features. She said, "Don't you know me, Ben?"

The stooped man's eyebrows raised. "Lady Clare Duncan!" he gasped.

"That's right," she said.

"But what are you doing here in America?"

"I have come to see your master," she said. "Is he at home?"

Again Ben looked unhappy. He hesitated. "Yes. I suppose he is to you. Do come inside, both of you." And he stood back for them to enter. As they did he told the agent, "You can carry in the luggage any time." Then he led them into a parlor to the right and sat the lamp on a table loaded with expensive ornaments. He indicated some easy chairs. "Do be seated, ladies."

Clare opened her purse. And taking out what she considered a suitable sum she passed it to Ben. "Will you kindly pay the driver for me?"

The old man bowed. "Of course, Lady Duncan." And he went out to look after this for her.

Belle was standing nervously by as Clare glanced around and inspected the room. From the small glow of the single lamp it was hard to tell much about it. Everything was in deep shadow except in their immediate area. But the room seemed to be elaborately furnished and the carpet under her feet was heavy. It had an air of staleness, as if it had gone for a long while without being used. Another flash of lightning showed through the windows and Belle gave a start.

Clare studied her worriedly. "You seem very much upset."

"I am nervous, my lady," the girl admitted.

"You mustn't be!" Clare cautioned her, knowing it was good advice but not able to take it herself. She was also on edge as the actual meeting with Barnabas approached. The obviously uneasy attitude of Ben had not helped things.

"I think it is the storm," Belle said forlornly.

"Quite likely it will pass without amounting to anything," she said. "And in any case we are quite safe here."

Ben came back into the room again with an apologetic air. "I have informed Mister Barnabas of your arrival," he said. "And he will be here shortly. In the meanwhile I will see that your things are taken upstairs and prepare rooms for you."

"Please don't put yourself out," Clare said.

"It will be largely makeshift, Lady Duncan. I trust you will take that into consideration. We have not been expecting visitors and few of the rooms have been made ready for use."

"It will be all right," Clare assured him.

The old man bowed and departed again. Clare began to worry if it wouldn't have been wiser for her and Belle to have first gone to the hotel. She could then have sent Barnabas a message of their arrival without bursting in on him in this manner. But it was too late to do anything about that now.

Belle had moved over to the big windows fronting on the

lawn and was staring nervously out into the dark night. She didn't like the way the pretty young girl was reacting to Stormcliff and the prospect of their meeting with Barnabas. Could it be that some of the power he'd held over her was still an active force?

There was a rustle of drapes and Clare turned quickly to see that Barnabas had come into the room through an archway at the other end of it. Now he stood there, a familiar figure in his Inverness coat and with his silver-headed cane in hand. He was no more than a dozen feet away and yet he made no move to come closer. His gaunt, handsome face wore an expression of great sadness.

At last he spoke. "Clare, why?"

Her pretty face was a study in emotions. All the mixed feelings this moment brought her being written there. In a resigned tone, she said, "I had to come, Barnabas. Since I truly love you, there was no other choice!"

"Clare, my darling!" the tall, courtly man said with deep emotion and now came to her. Taking her in his arms, he pressed her close to him.

"I hope you're not angry, Barnabas," she said, tears of happiness brimming in her eyes.

He cupped his hand under her chin and turned her face up to his. There was great gentleness in his face and in his manner. "Of course I'm not angry, my darling," he said. "Your coming half-a-world to join me is a tribute I do not deserve. But I am surprised and troubled. Troubled for you."

"It was what I wanted to do, Barnabas. Neither father nor anyone else could stop me."

"I would have tried to if I had known," he said, a light of seriousness coming into his hypnotic eyes.

"Why, Barnabas?" she pleased.

"I think by this time you know why," he said quietly and with a significance that was like a chill wind sweeping around her.

"That doesn't matter," she protested. "We will find a way."

Barnabas smiled sadly. "You make me want to believe that."

"You must believe it," she said.

He sighed. "We can discuss that later. You must be weary. Ben is making up some kind of accommodation for you. This old house has only recently been opened. Much of it has been unused for a long while."

"Please don't fuss over us," Clare protested. And with a smile she turned to indicate Belle who was still standing a distance off by the window looking ill at ease. "You see who I brought with me as a traveling companion."

Barnabas now gave his attention to the attractive maid. He seemed completely surprised. "Belle!" he said. "So you came along as well!"

"Lady Duncan insisted that I should," Belle said meekly.

He smiled at Clare. "You chose well in selecting her," he said. "Belle is a fine girl."

"I was sure you'd approve," Clare said. She hesitated. "I felt it ought to be someone who knew you and understood you."

Barnabas turned his eyes to Belle again. "I'm sure she does that," he said with meaning. "I would like to entertain you ladies but I have an appointment in the village I must keep."

Clare gave him an anxious, pleading look. "There are so many things to discuss. Can't you stay here?"

Barnabas shook his head. "I regret that it is of a pressing nature," he said.

There was a rumble of thunder, louder than any before, and Clare studied him with worried eyes. "In any case, it is going to storm."

"I'm not troubled by storms," Barnabas said impassively. "I'm sure you are aware of that."

Clare frowned. "The man who drove us here told us some strange stories. He said there had been weird happenings in the village lately."

"Really?" Barnabas regarded her with almost a coldness. His mood had so swiftly changed.

But Clare felt she must go on whether she angered him or not. It was for his good. She said, "According to him a girl was strangled in a field to the rear of the local bar. A girl of easy virtue, the sort who would readily become friendly with strangers. And the townspeople are greatly upset over it."

"Why mention this to me?" Barnabas asked.

"I wondered if you'd heard about it."

"I have."

"And there was something else," she forced herself to add, knowing that he might hate her for it, but also realizing there must be honesty between them from now on or they would have no hope of building a future. "Several other girls have suffered attacks by a mysterious stranger. Fortunately they were lucky enough to escape unharmed."

"So?" he said.

"I know how fond you are of wandering about alone at night," she went on. "And I began to worry that the local people might suspect you of being the mysterious stranger. You haven't been here long. And these people wouldn't understand you." She felt she had been tactful enough.

Barnabas offered her a cool smile. "I think you are worrying yourself needlessly. If these people suspected me they could have come to me some time ago. Since they haven't, I would imagine they have never thought of me in that regard."

"I'm sorry," she said. "I mentioned it only for your good."

"That is one of the problems between us," he said. "What you consider beneficial to me is not always that. And I must confess there are many occasions on which I am far from understanding you. This being one of them."

"We should not quarrel on this first meeting in months," she pleaded.

"I have no thought of quarreling," the handsome Barnabas said with a strange gleam in his hypnotic eyes. "You might do better to model yourself after Belle, who greets me with proper modesty and silence."

And with that he bowed to them both and quickly left the big room. Clare stood there feeling lost. He was going to be no easier to deal with than he had before. And his anger at her reference to what had been happening in the village seemed to confirm her worst fears.

The front door opened and was slammed shut. The echo of it rang through the old mansion. Clare gave a tiny shudder. It was as if Barnabas Collins had slammed the door closed on all her hopes. Had she come so far on a futile mission? Would Barnabas refuse to try and help himself?

Belle came close to her, her pretty face pale. "I'm sure he did not mean a half of what he said," the girl suggested in a small voice.

Clare gave her a thoughtful glance. "Perhaps he spoke a great truth," she admitted. "It is possible that he considers you have been a better friend to him than I have ever been."

"That is not so!" the girl protested.

"You do not realize to what extent you have played a part in his life and well-being," Clare assured her. "And for your peace of mind it is best that you don't."

The thunder came again and with it a tremendous flash of lightning. And then the rain came pouring down. Belle stood there looking lost and frightened. Clare felt sorry for the girl and for herself as well.

She said, "We'll stay a few days and see what can be accomplished. Then perhaps we'll go back to England."

"Your father would welcome you, but he will also be very angry," Belle said.

Clare smiled bitterly. "He'd get over his anger but he'd never cease to taunt me for following the promptings of my foolish heart."

Ben came back to join them. "The rooms are ready, Lady Duncan. At least as ready as I can make them at short notice. The linen is clean and I have lit fires in both fireplaces to dispel the chill."

"Thank you, Ben," Clare said. "That is kind of you."

"If you will follow me," he invited them. And they went out into the hallway and up a broad, steep flight of stairs. At the top he turned and led them down a carpeted hallway. He paused at an open door. "This is your ladyship's room. Your companion's is the one next to it. And there is a connecting door between them."

"Thank you, Ben," Clare said, glancing into the room which was to be hers and grateful for the pleasant fire which was already filling the bedchamber with a welcome warmth. The old stone house had a chill about it.

As Ben moved on to escort Belle to her room, Clare went into the bedroom assigned to her and saw her bags were all properly spread out and ready to unpack. The bed was a solid one of carved mahogany, no doubt imported by the first owner of the house from Europe. But there were signs of neglect about that could not be ignored. The handsome enameled-base lamp with its frosted pink chimney which Ben had sat on the dresser cast a soft illumination over most of the high-ceilinged area.

Combined with the brisk fire's reflection it showed up nearly every corner of the bedroom. And it seemed a kind of protection from the storm that was raging outside. Moving across to the dresser, she studied her reflection in the mirror. The cape she was wearing covered all her dress and was not flattering to her. Its dark crimson made the whiteness of her skin stand out and the black shadows of weariness under her eyes seem deeper. She showed the effects of her long journey.

She looked up and saw that Ben had not gotten around to dusting the room. A large, finely spun spider's web stretched between the upper right post of the mirror and the wall. In its center was the fat spider and creator of the trap; its hapless victims were caught at various points in the outer portions of the web. There they remained, pale and dried-up, forlorn remnants of what had been living creatures once.

Could the spider and the web have a symbolic meaning for her? Was it a warning she would best not ignore? The medium had told her she would never find happiness with Barnabas and she'd refused to believe him. Now it seemed he might have been right.

There was a hesitant knock on her door. She went over and opened it to discover the stooped Ben standing there. The old servant wore an expression of embarrassment on his hollow-cheeked, bearded face.

He said, "May I have a word with your ladyship in private?"

She stared at him. The thunder sounded outside again. "Why, yes, if you like." And she moved back for him to enter.

When she closed the door he hesitated a moment before saying, "I regret you did not receive too warm a welcome from my master."

"He did not seem his usual self," she said, feeling that Ben had something he wanted to tell her. And she was afraid to hear it.

Ben licked his thin lips nervously. "The truth is that Mr. Barnabas is in deep trouble," he said in an earnest tone. "He has fallen completely under the spell of a deceitful and dangerous woman. I'm afraid he is forever lost to you, Lady Duncan."

CHAPTER 8

Her inner turmoil matched that of the storm outside. She had been aware of a subtle difference in the way Barnabas behaved toward her, but she had not guessed another woman was involved. Rather, she had blamed it on the terrible curse which caused his need to restore himself with fresh human blood regardless of what it involved.

She gave the old servant a sharp glance. "You are certain of this?"

"Only too certain," he sighed. "When I first saw you at the door tonight it seemed like a stroke of good fortune. Perhaps you had come in time to save him. But you see how it is? He has gone off to her as he does every night."

"Do you believe he really loves her?"

"She has made him think so," Ben said unhappily. "Her name is Julia Conrad. Her husband is a captain who has made his home in this town. He has a three-masted schooner, the *Belle Corliss*, which he sails between here and the West Indies. He is away a good deal of the time and his wife has gained the reputation of being unfaithful to him."

"This before Barnabas came along?"

"Oh, yes, Lady Duncan. Julia Conrad has long used her charm and beauty to attract men in her husband's absence. Naturally,

Mister Barnabas presented a challenge to her. And she has ensnared him just as she'd done with many others."

Clare was shocked. So this was what she had to face along with the curse under which Barnabas suffered! She said, "Does thisJulia Conrad know the truth about Barnabas as I do?"

Ben hesitated. "I'm not sure I'm aware of what you mean, my lady."

Her eyes met his in a grim glance. "I saw his coffin in his flat in London. And I saw you help him into it. I also know what happened to Eileen O'Mara and how he feasted on those other girls. I know that Barnabas is a vampire."

There was a roar of thunder and lightning blazed in the window, giving the room an eerie brightness for a second. Ben gave her a wary look. "That is dangerous knowledge, Lady Duncan."

"I do not plan to use it against him or you," she said. "Not unless I find it necessary for the protection of innocents. Did he murder that girl whose body they found?"

He licked his lips again. "I don't think so. I'm not sure. They tell she was strangled."

"And her blood drained?"

"It could be, but I somehow doubt it," Ben said. "I can generally tell when my master is mixed up in anything of that sort. I believe he has preyed on some of the village girls for blood, but I don't think it has gone further than that."

"Does he leave his mark on the neck of this Julia Conrad? Is she feeding him with her blood as well as false love?" Clare asked with scorn.

Ben spread his hands. "I think there is a close link between them and that is likely it. He seldom loses his head to a woman. You were the last one I feel sure he truly loved. But now there is this new woman."

The lightning came again but not for so long, nor was it so bright. The rain lashed the windows with new fury. Clare said, "So I have made my long journey for nothing?"

"I hope not," Ben said. "I only pray that you may be able to reason with him. I doubt this Julia will show him the same consideration when she knows the truth."

"And she must find it out eventually," Clare reminded him.

"That is my constant fear," Ben worried. "I have watched this happening knowing that it must end in disaster."

"Perhaps her husband will come home soon and break it up."

"His ship is due shortly," Ben said. "I have checked on that. But I see no hope there. She has deceived him too many times before, if local talk is to be believed."

"Then it could end with a stake through Barnabas' heart,"

Clare said. "That is the way they deal with vampires, isn't it?"

Ben turned a deathly shade of gray. "Pray do not talk of such things."

"Dr. Fontaine is no more. He came to his end that way," Clare informed the stooped man calmly.

The stooped man crossed himself. "Somehow he must be saved from his folly. I felt it my duty to tell you."

"I will try and reason with him," she said. "Where does this woman live?"

"In a cottage on the road to the village," Ben said. "You would have passed it on the drive here tonight. It is white and is partially hidden from the road by a tall row of lilac bushes."

"I'll remember," she promised.

"I trust you will be comfortable here, Lady Duncan," Ben said. "It is the best I was able to do at such brief notice." With a bow he left her, the discreet servant again now that his lapse was over.

The thunder and lightning came fainter and more distant now, although the rain continued heavily. The storm was moving on. She was still standing there, weary and dejected, studying the flames in the fireplace disconsolately, when the door between her room and Belle's creaked open. She turned to see the pretty dark-haired girl standing there in her nightgown.

There was fear on Belle's face as she asked, "May I help you in any way, my lady?"

"Thank you, no," Clare said. "I can manage nicely alone."

The girl hesitated. "I believe the storm is over."

"Yes," Clare said. And taking a step over to her she added, "You seem upset?"

"I'm sorry," Belle said, glancing down. "It was the storm, I think."

"And seeing Mister Barnabas again?"

Belle looked up at her with frightened eyes. "I don't know. It did make me feel strange. And he was so different. So cruel."

"You must remember that Barnabas is a very complex person with many problems of which we're not even aware," she said. "Try to forget about it and get a good night's sleep."

"Yes, my lady," Belle said. And with another uneasy glance her way the pretty maid quickly left the room.

Clare found additional cause for alarm in Belle's edgy state. She was convinced that Barnabas was responsible. She had not yet had time to talk to him about the girl. But she would as soon as she conveniently could. And she would be emphatic that he leave Belle alone. Let him find the blood he needed other places. Let him feast on the throat of that Julia Conrad more often. If she wanted to be wooed by one of the living dead she should be willing to pay the price.

With these bitter thoughts Clare slowly prepared for bed. Because of her weariness and the heat from the fireplace she almost at once dropped into a sleep of deep exhaustion. It was a dreamless sleep in which she hardly stirred.

When she finally awoke with a start the room was in almost complete darkness. Only a small glow from the embers in the fireplace cut through the shadows. And there standing at the foot of her bed was the caped figure of Barnabas!

Clare sat up with a small cry of alarm, the bedclothes pressed against her. "What are you doing here?"

"I came to watch you while you slept," he said with a gentle sadness.

"Barnabas, you must try to save yourself!"

"It is much too late for that," he said with a bitter smile. "A century too late."

"I refuse to believe that," she said. "The curse can be broken by love."

"It has been tried before and failed."

"That woman, that Julia," Clare said. "She cannot help you. Her kind of love is not lasting or she would be faithful to her husband."

The gaunt, handsome face showed consternation. "How did you find out about Julia?"

"It doesn't matter how," she said. "I'm warning you she'll be no good for you. She doesn't love you the way I do—doesn't know about the curse!"

He shrugged and shifted his silver-headed cane from one hand to the other, "It is because she doesn't know that I can love her. Just as I loved you until you discovered my secret."

She leaned forward in the bed, urgency on her pretty face. "But you're all wrong in that. The fact my love has survived discovering the truth about you proves it to be real. I have come all this way to help you, feeling that you were close to me the whole time. I will make any sacrifice for you, Barnabas."

He smiled, revealing the perfect white teeth beneath his thick lips. "Including giving me up to Julia Conrad?"

She sighed. "I suppose I would even do that if I thought it would save you. But falling under her spell is a mistake."

Barnabas stood very straight, the black hair plastered about his forehead from the wet. He said, "Julia makes me feel like a normal human being. Can you understand what that means to me?"

"I don't know," she confessed.

"To you I'm a pitiful creature," he went on. "One of the living dead. And since you're not among those who despise me you show sympathy for me. That is what it has to be now, Clare. Sympathy, not love! You want to save me! You don't talk about loving me as Julia does!"

"It proves my love is of a deeper and better kind!" she pleaded.

"It shows you have a kind heart," Barnabas said with bitterness. "But it doesn't hide the fact that you will never regard me in the same way as when I courted you."

"I was a little fool then! I knew nothing!"

"Better to be a little fool than have evil wisdom," Barnabas told her. "You can best make me happy by leaving here and forgetting me altogether."

"That's impossible!"

Barnabas stared at her with concern. "I'm thinking of you as much or more than I am myself. For though things are different now, I do still love you. If you remain here we may destroy what love we knew and our very selves."

"I can't go without at least trying to do something for you."

"And I cannot send you away," Barnabas said sadly. "So there is our predicament. Now only Julia has the chance to save me. Will you enjoy remaining and seeing me court her?"

"Her husband will soon return. Then you will have no choice but to leave her alone."

"No. He does not care. He no longer loves her," Barnabas said. "I have it from her own lips."

"And I would pay scant attention to that," Clare said scathingly. "Women of her type are always liars."

"Try to understand," Barnabas pleaded. "In the name of the love we shared."

"Don't ask for that kind of promise," Clare said unhappily.

"Give it some thought," Barnabas said. "And I'm certain you'll realize you can best help me by leaving here as soon as possible."

Clare had another thought, prompted by his very vitality. She gave him an accusing look. "Did you first make a visit to the other room before coming here to me?"

Barnabas hesitated. "Why do you ask?"

"You seem so refreshed, none of your usual weariness," she went on. "Did you pause along the way to feast on Belle's blood?"

His gaunt, handsome face showed strain. "That is not a fair question."

"I knew you had!" she said. "Otherwise she would have heard us before this and been in here! I warn you, Barnabas, I did not bring that girl here for you to harm her."

"I mean her no harm," he said uneasily.

"But you have become accustomed to her blood," Clare went

on. "You cannot easily forget how pleasant it tasted in London! Well, you must forget! I forbid you to molest her again!"

"You have no proof that I have touched her," Barnabas countered.

"That will not take long to discover!" Clare told him as she swung out of bed and into her slippers and then raced across the room to the door connecting to Belle's bedroom.

The dark-haired girl lay sprawled under the bedclothes, her head at an angle on the pillow. She seemed in a deep sleep. There was enough light from the fireplace to see a little and as Clare leaned forward the telltale red mark was visible on the girl's shapely white throat. And there seemed to be a single drop of blood staining the pillow. Clare stared down at her in horror and revulsion. She had brought the girl to this!

She turned and went back to her own bedchamber, but as she closed the door behind her she saw that Barnabas was gone. He had not been able to stay and face her.

The next morning was bright and sunny. Belle, though looking pale, seemed none the worse for Barnabas' visit in the night. As soon as Clare had breakfasted she made a routine inspection of the imposing stone mansion. It was larger than she had realized in the darkness of the night before. She had more than just a casual interest in inspecting the various rooms. She was anxious to discover where Barnabas rested during the daylight hours.

A thorough inspection of the upper floors revealed no locked rooms. The house was dusty and damp from being closed so long, but its condition in no way matched the grime of the strange castle on Mont St. Michel where Dr. Fontaine had held forth. It would not take a great deal of work to put Stormcliff in good condition. But with Ben the only servant, it was not likely the place would get much attention.

The only possible place left for Barnabas to have his lair, and the most likely one, was the cellar. Ben was nowhere in sight when she found her way to the entrance to the cellar. It was through the big kitchen at the rear of the house. A stone flight of steps led directly down to the dank lower level of storage and foundation. She had fortified herself with a lighted candle and with it held high she made her way along a narrow corridor with an earthen floor. On each side there were roughly partitioned areas. And at the very end of the corridor there was a wooden door with a padlock on it. She was reasonably sure that Barnabas slept in his coffin beyond that door.

She was standing there with the lighted candle in hand when she heard a footstep behind her. Wheeling around, she came face to face with Ben. The stooped man did not seem pleased to see her there.

"Yes, Lady Duncan?" he questioned her.

"You startled me," she told him.

"I hardly expected to find you down here," was his reply.

"I've been trying to find where Barnabas spends his days. It is down here in that locked room, isn't it?"

"He would not like me discussing this with you," Ben reminded her.

"I understand," she said. "I just wanted to know for my own reasons."

"Then there is nothing else you want down here?" His tone was not exactly friendly and his words were an invitation for her to leave and go back upstairs.

"No. I suppose not," she said with a final glance at the locked door.

She returned to the stone steps and made her way up to the kitchen with Ben on her heels. And when they got up there she noticed that he carefully locked the door leading to the cellar as well.

Snuffing out the candle and placing the holder on the kitchen table, she asked him, "Can I get a conveyance to take me to the village?"

"We have nothing here. Only over at Collinwood."

"I see," she said. "And it is a long walk."

"Too long for you, my lady," the stooped old man said in his dry way. "It doesn't bother the village folk. They are used to it."

She said, "I should like to call on that Mrs. Julia Conrad. I might be able to reason with her."

Ben sallow face showed concern. "I do not advise that," he said. "I can see nothing but harm resulting from such a meeting. I should not have spoken to you about that business at all. But I have been badly worried. Last night my tongue was too loose."

"And Barnabas reprimanded you for telling me," she suggested.

He looked down at the stone floor. "I would prefer that you forget I said anything."

"Very well. If that is what you wish."

The old man seemed afraid. "You do not understand. He has ways of knowing things, of hearing what is said even though he's in that coffin down there in the darkness. He can be a Devil when he likes."

Clare was sympathetic. "I don't want to put you in an awkward position, Ben. I'll not bring the subject up again."

"Thank you, Lady Duncan," he said humbly.

She left the kitchen to go on the grounds and stroll in the sun. Ben's abject attitude this morning was in great contrast to his manner of the night before. Barnabas had undoubtedly reprimanded him.

And there seemed no question that he feared the powers his master possessed. The interview had depressed her.

Coming here with such high hopes and good intentions it was not pleasant to have made the discoveries she had during her first few hours in the old house. From the front lawn of the stone mansion there was an excellent view of the ocean. And on the right Collinwood stood on a hill not more than a few minutes' walk away. She regretted that the other members of the Collins family were not at home. She might have gotten valuable information and aid from them.

She discovered a narrow grass-grown road which led to Collinwood and began walking along it in the direction of the house. She had not gone more than a dozen yards when she saw a wagon drawn by two horses leave the barn of Collinwood and come along the road in her direction. She stepped to one side of the road, waiting until it reached her.

The driver of the wagon wore a battered straw hat and was a young man in his late teens or early twenties. He had a round, good-natured face covered with freckles and a heavy tan. His clothing was shabby, but he held the reins on the gray pair proudly. When she waved to him he brought the horses to a halt.

Shading her eyes from the sun with her hand, she asked, "Are you going to Collinsport?"

"Most all the way," he said in a youthful voice.

"Will you pass the Conrad cottage?"

"Captain Will Conrad's place?" the boy asked.

"Yes."

"Have to pass it. It's the first house along the road."

"Would you take me there?"

The youth registered surprise. "A lady like you wants to ride on a rig like this?"

"I don't mind if you'd be kind enough to give me a lift."

The youth glanced back over his shoulder in the direction of Collinwood. "I don't guess the boss would mind," he said. With a grin he leaned over and reached out a bronzed hand. "It's a big step up here, miss."

It was. But she had wide skirts even if they trailed the ground and so she accepted his offered hand and balanced herself to spring up on the wagon beside him. She managed it gracefully and seated herself with a smile.

"Thank you," she said. "It's very good of you. Will you be coming back this way?"

"In about two hours," he said. "I've got to get some provisions in Collinsport. And there's a set of harness waiting at the blacksmith shop I'm to take back."

"I may be walking home," she said. "If you overtake me I might get a ride part of the way home."

"If you don't mind it one way I guess you wouldn't mind the other," he said with another friendly grin. "You the new maid at Stormcliff?"

"No. I'm just a visitor."

He looked impressed. "You a friend of that Barnabas Collins? You talk sort of like him."

She smiled. "You mean we both have British accents."

"Yep. I guess that's it. You sure don't talk like the folks around here."

"I know Mr. Collins very well. We met in London."

"He's a right strange one," was the boy's opinion. "No one ever sees a sign of him until after dark—and there are stories that he wanders around the whole night. The housekeeper at Collinwood was up with a sore tooth and she looked out her window at about three o'clock in the morning and saw him strolling by moonlight in the Collins' private cemetery. She can see it easy from her room on the top floor."

Clare said. "How could she be certain it was Barnabas Collins?"

"He was wearing that funny coat with a cape on it. No one else has a coat like that around here."

"I see," she said. "Of course with her tooth paining and it being so late she could have been mistaken."

"Maybe," the youth admitted. "But there's something odd about that Barnabas just the same. Him and that servant living all alone in the house until you arrived. And I don't guess he's too welcome over at Collinwood."

"All his relatives at Collinwood are away."

"Maybe they wanted to be away," the boy suggested. "From what I hear, a long time ago his grandfather left here in bad trouble. He was told not to come back. His folks didn't want him around."

"I hadn't heard that," she said.

They were rounding the corner of a road wooded on both sides. But now they were coming to cleared ground. And on the right she saw a house set back from the road and fronted by lilac bushes.

"That's the Conrad place," he said, reining the grays.

She thanked him and managed a precarious descent from the wagon by herself, scraping her ankle a little on the edge of the big iron-rimmed wheel. He waved to her as he drove on and she waved back. Her conversation with him had confirmed what she'd suspected: Barnabas was treading on thin ice. The local people were already talking about him and it wouldn't take long for them to start blaming him for some of the unpleasant midnight incidents that had happened of late.

Brushing the dust off her plain gray dress, she slowly made her way up the path that led to the rather small cottage occupied by Captain Will Conrad and his wife, Julia. She had no idea what she intended to say to the woman since she'd had no time to think about it. The ride had come as a lucky chance and she'd seized on it before she'd planned any strategy. In a moment she would be meeting the woman who had captured the interest of Barnabas to such an extent that he was willing to throw aside all his usual caution.

She lifted the brass knob ring on the front door and rapped just loudly enough so that it might be heard. Then she waited. The sun was strong and she regretted she hadn't brought along a parasol. She feared she had received a sunburn riding in the open on the wagon seat.

She heard footsteps approaching the door and a moment later it was opened by a slim, willowy woman with a pouting, pretty face, olive skin and brownish hair.

"Yes?" she said.

"Are you Mrs. Conrad? Mrs. Julia Conrad?"

"I am." The large brown eyes of the woman regarded her with suspicion.

"You don't know me," Clare said carefully. "But I wanted to meet you."

Julia Conrad frowned. "Who are you?"

"A visitor from England. I'm a friend of Barnabas Collins."

The woman's manner became somewhat more amiable. "Did Barnabas send you here?"

"Not really," she said. "But we did discuss you."

"Oh?" Julia was at once wary again.

"May I come inside and talk with you for a little?" Clare asked politely.

The woman hesitated. "I still don't know who you are."

"My name is Clare Duncan. And I knew Barnabas in London."

Julia Conrad still stared at her with suspicious eyes. "All right, you can visit for a little," she said. "I have other company coming later."

Clare entered the shadowed, cool front parlor and wondered if it was some other man Julia was expecting. "I only plan to ask a few minutes of your time."

The other woman looked relieved. She waved to a wingback chair. "Sit down," she said.

Clare seated herself. "I hope you won't think I'm intruding," she said. "But I've come to see you as a friend of Barnabas. I understand you and he have been spending a lot of time in each other's company."

The pretty Julia bridled. "I don't know who's been telling you that," she exclaimed. "But I can tell you it's none of your business."

"You're quite right," Clare agreed in a quiet voice. "And yet I want to help Barnabas and spare you some hurt if I can." She paused "I think you should be told that Barnabas is not a well man."

Julia glared at her. "He seems healthy enough to me."

"You know that he goes out only after the sun sets?"

"It's his way. He keeps busy with his books during the day. Barnabas is a scholar," Julia said proudly. "That's nothing to be ashamed of."

"That's not his chief reason for only appearing in the hours of darkness," Clare said, at the same time straining to see if there might be any identifying red marks on Julia's throat. She saw a mottled place that could well be the remains of such a mark.

"Then what is his reason?" Julia asked.

"He fears the daylight," Clare told her. "It is part of his illness. There can be no lasting happiness for you with him."

"I don't know what you're talking about," Julia said indignantly. "I happen to be a married woman."

"I know about that. And I'm warning you just the same. You'd be wise to break off with Barnabas."

Julia eyed her with a sarcastic smile. "Why? So you can have him?"

"I can help him if you will allow it. But you must stop seeing him, for both your sakes."

Julia rose with a sneer. "You want my answer to that?"

Clare got to her feet. "I suppose I do. That's what I came here for."

"You wasted your time," the woman said. "Nobody will stop me from seeing Barnabas! Nobody!"

CHAPTER 9

Because she had remained in the Conrad cottage such a short while, she was forced to walk the entire distance back to Stormcliff. It took her almost two hours and she was both tired and dusty by the time she got back. But she had gained something from the solitary journey. It had given her time to think.

The meeting with Julia Conrad had shown her there was no hope of cooperation from her. Julia seemed to have no hint that Barnabas was one of the living dead. To her, he was a novelty. A scholar and a man of charm was obviously a rarity in Collinsport and it pleased Julia to think she had made an easy conquest of him.

Neither did Barnabas seem to be in a mood for reason. This had surprised her. But she could see that with his hurt pride he found some consolation in rejecting her. He was afraid she pitied rather than loved him and unless she could convince him otherwise he would continue to turn his back on her. The chances against her helping him now seemed truly formidable.

It seemed to her the only hope rested with Captain Will Conrad. If he should turn out to be a reasonable man she could reveal what was going on between Barnabas and his wife, without having to tell him the truth about Barnabas, and ask him to break up the affair. The easiest way would be for him to take his wife from the local scene—perhaps on a voyage with him, as so many of the local sea captains did with their wives. It was the best possible solution and with the *Belle Corliss* returning to port within a few days, she would soon find out if the captain would listen to her.

With this decided she went into the house. After she had rested she had Belle help her bring out a tin bathtub from the closet and fill it with lukewarm water. When she had bathed she felt much better and selected the dress she would be wearing for the late afternoon and evening. She decided on a blue silk. Barnabas had always liked that color on her. She hoped he still would.

Ben served them a simple dinner of local haddock with new potatoes and string beans. The food was merely passable; the old servant was not a skilled cook. But Clare could hardly complain, since she had forced her company and that of Belle's on Barnabas. Dinner was a quiet affair with Belle noticeably on edge again and speaking only when she was spoken to.

Clare was not immune to the ominous atmosphere hovering over the great stone house either. As sunset arrived she wandered out across the lawn to the cliff's edge. Far below the waves dashed against the rocky shore. It was a wild, rugged stretch of seacoast. With the sinking sun the night took on a tinge of blue. The monotonous breaking of the waves made her uneasy. She turned to walk back to the house to discover Barnabas striding across the lawn to join her.

He made a noble figure in his Inverness coat and the black cane swung gracefully in step with him. But his handsome face was set in a stern expression as he came up to her.

Halting a few feet from where she stood near the cliff's edge, he said, "You did something today that I wish you hadn't."

She pretended innocence. "I don't follow you."

"You saw Julia."

She was startled. "What makes you think that?"

"I know," he said with those hypnotic eyes fixed on her. "You must have realized she wouldn't listen to you. She wouldn't have if you'd told her the whole truth. And you didn't."

"I wanted to see the kind of person she was. She's not worthy of you, Barnabas."

He smiled bitterly. "Are you in a fair position to offer that judgment?"

She felt her cheeks burn. "Yes. I think so. I'm trying to be very fair in this. She thinks she has won herself a great gentleman and a scholar. She's too stupid to notice there is something different about you."

Barnabas arched an eyebrow. "As I recall, a certain unnamed lady in London wasn't too quick to realize that either. And when she did it was chiefly through the shrewd guessing and prodding of her father. Am I right, Lady Duncan?"

"I was slow in finding out the truth about you," she admitted, feeling shamed and unhappy. "But when I did discover what you are my feelings toward you didn't change. I still love you, Barnabas."

The gaunt, handsome face took on a forgiving expression. He came closer to her and took her in his arms. And this time he touched his lips to her forehead and she couldn't restrain a tiny shiver since those lips were ice cold!

Barnabas released her with an oath. "So you see how it is in spite of your protestations? You find me repulsive, regardless of your noble words."

"That's not so!" she insisted.

"Your behavior just now spoke far more eloquently than anything you can say," Barnabas told her. "It is too late for us. Why shouldn't I turn to Julia?"

"It's not too late! You can be cured! First, you must break yourself of your thirst for blood."

He stared at her with disbelief on his gaunt, handsome face. "How can you ask me that, knowing that without fresh human blood I'll wither and die?"

"It would be the first step in a return to normalcy," she insisted. "You can manage if you resolve not to taste blood again. It is the one thing about you that I detest."

"You would rather see me die?"

"I don't think it would come to that. I can't bear to think of your preying on innocents like Belle. How can you bring yourself to do it?"

"See it from my point of view," he said. "I must do it to survive."

"Is it that important to survive as you are?"

"The urge to survive is a strong one regardless of one's condition. You may find that out one day. When you have lived a century, as I have, things take on a different perspective."

Clare studied him sadly. "I fear you have become extremely selfish."

"I have my weaknesses," he was ready to admit. "And one of them being lovely women, I must be on my way to meet Julia again."

"You say that to mock me!" she accused him. "To hurt me!" Dusk was closing in on them. Their faces were veiled and she could no longer clearly read his expression.

He shrugged. "I may be mocking you, dear lady. But that is merely a protective attitude on my part. You know what I am and it disgusts you. I try to let you see that I don't care what you think. But I'm not deliberately out to hurt you."

"What difference? It amounts to the same thing in the end."

"I ask you once again to give up this hopeless plan you have in your pretty head," he begged her. "Take Belle and leave here before tragedy follows on tragedy. I shall not be responsible for what happens if you insist on remaining."

"And I shall consider myself a coward if I leave," she said resolutely.

"There is an old saying," Barnabas told her, "that tells us to let the dead rest. I think you should ponder on it." And with that he turned and strode off into the darkness.

She remained where she was at the cliff's edge, the waves in the dark below beating a mournful dirge to her hopes as they crashed on the rocks. She knew there was much truth in what he had just said. But still she could not bring herself to admit defeat. Not yet!

The *Belle Corliss* came into port two days later. Ben told Clare and at once she was eager to visit the ship. She walked over to Collinwood and arranged with the stableman to have the use of a carriage for the afternoon. He gave her a light one-seater and a placid brown mare. Since she'd had a carriage of her own back in London she was no stranger to the reins.

She actually enjoyed the drive in to the small village of Collinsport. She drove the carriage down the hilly main street and tied the horse to a post near the docks. Then she walked the rest of the way to the wharf where the *Belle Corliss* was being unloaded. The cargo seemed to have consisted chiefly of huge wooden casks of molasses. The sweet sticky stuff had oozed out of the joints of the casks and the whole area smelled of it.

Sturdy Maine fishing types along with several burly men who appeared to make up part of the crew were bending their backs to the business of unloading the casks on the wharf. Amid ship a sturdy, bronzed man in his thirties wearing a nautical peaked cap over a head of curly, brown hair gave sharp orders to the workers. Since he was obviously in command of things she assumed he was Captain Conrad. So she walked up the two planks running from ship to shore and across the deck to where he stood.

He paused in his shouting to study her with some perplexity. "What it is, miss?"

"Are you Captain Will Conrad?" she asked.

He shook his head. "No, miss. The captain went ashore for a few minutes. He'll be back soon. I'm the first mate, Nathan

Forbes. Can I help you in any way?"

She hesitated. "I'm afraid I must see him. It's a personal matter." She glanced around her. "You have a fine ship."

"She does well enough," Nathan Forbes agreed. "She's just short of two hundred feet long. A good size for a three-master plying the Indies trade."

"Do you like the sea?"

"Followed it since I was ten," he said. "If you're going to wait for the captain, let me take you to his cabin. This is pretty busy out here."

She hesitated. "I don't want to be a bother."

"It's a pleasure, miss," he said with a pleasant smile. He led the way aft to the cabin area of the stately schooner.

Clare was impressed by the young man. His manners were excellent and while his education must be limited since he'd followed the sea since he was a boy of ten, he did not show the lack of it. He opened the door to a cabin and stood aside for her to enter.

It was small but elaborately paneled in fine wood and equipped with a rolltop desk and other suitable articles of furniture. She turned to smile at the young man. "This is very nice," she said.

"The *Belle Corliss* is a well built ship," Nathan Forbes said. "And nothing was stinted on the quarters of master, officers or crew. Her tonnage is close to eight hundred so she is a good size for the trade. Larger than most."

"You must take pride in her," Clare said, "since she is your home a good deal of the time."

He nodded cheerfully. "Most of our days are spent aboard."

"Do you not find it monotonous?"

"Not for me," Forbts said. "I do a deal of reading. Each voyage I load up with a packet of books. It fills in for my lack of formal schooling."

"So that's the secret," she said. "I wondered."

"The first captain I shipped out with was a fine scholar and he took an interest in my welfare," Nathan Forbes told her.

Clare had seated herself in a plain chair across from the desk. "And what is Captain Conrad like?"

The young man looked surprised. "You've never met him?"

"No."

"I took it for granted you had," he said. "You mentioned wanting to talk to him on a personal matter."

Clare found herself blushing. Much of her assurance was leaving her under the serious scrutiny of the young man. She said, "I do wish to discuss a matter important to me and I believe also to him," she said lamely.

Nathan Forbes's blue eyes searched her face. "A personal matter," he repeated. And then he surprised her completely by gravely suggesting, "I guess this would have something to do about his wife, Julia."

She looked up at him in surprise. "How did you guess that?"

He looked grimly resigned. "You're not the first worried female to come here and try to talk to the captain about Julia. Other wives have been here to complain about straying husbands."

Her blushing continued furiously. "I'm not married, Mr. Forbes."

"I didn't notice your hand," he apologized. "Well, wife, sister or what have you, I can guarantee you're not the first to board the *Belle Corliss* with a problem concerning Julia. And I must warn you it won't do any good."

"Why do you say that?"

"Because I know it to be so," the young man assured her. "Captain Conrad is a stubborn man. He knows the sort of woman Julia is but he won't admit it to himself and certainly not to others. Because of her misguided actions he has become a silent, bitter man. A man not to be approached in a matter of this kind."

She got up from the chair. "Then I had better go."

"I'm sorry to have to tell you this. But I wanted to spare you further embarrassment," the first mate said earnestly. "Captain Conrad can be cruel on occasion."

"Thank you for your interest," she said and took a step toward the cabin door.

Nathan Forbes stood by the door partially blocking her way. "I have a suggestion."

"Yes?" She was too upset to be much interested.

"I am probably Captain Conrad's best friend as well as being first mate of the *Belle Corliss*," Nathan Forbes said earnestly. "I have his confidence more than most people. If you'd care to confide what's troubling you to me I'd be willing to do what I can to help."

Clare studied his frank, bronzed face and somehow knew that this man could be a good friend to her. And she was in sore need of someone to turn to.

She said, "It's very difficult. There is a man new to Collinsport. A man you would not know. His name is Barnabas Collins."

Nathan Forbes gave a low whistle. "That name has a familiar ring. I've read some histories of this town. If I'm not mistaken there was a Barnabas Collins lived here long ago. He felt under the shadow of some dark business. Witchcraft or something like that. Is this Barnabas Collins a descendant of his by any chance?"

"There is a relationship," she said carefully. "Barnabas Collins came here from London months back. He became acquainted with Julia Conrad and now he's madly infatuated with her. I'm afraid she's given him every encouragement. The difficulty is that Barnabas Collins is a very sick man. And this kind of alliance could cost him his very existence."

The young bronzed face registered interest. "You make a strong case of it, miss," he said. "I take it you are vitally interested since you are English yourself. Could it be you are or were engaged to this Barnabas Collins?"

She sighed. She was beyond embarrassment at this point, only her concern for Barnabas had importance. "You are right. I was engaged to Barnabas. But that is over. Now I only wish to help him. And because of his illness he desperately needs help."

"What sort of illness does he have?" the young man said with understandable curiosity.

Clare found herself caught in a trap of her own making. She did not have sufficient confidence in the young man yet to tell him the whole truth. She countered with, "It is both a mental and a physical deterioration. He needs special care."

"I see," he said dubiously. "And why did you come to talk to the captain? How did you expect he could help? Certainly it would do no good for him to tell Julia to stop seeing this man. She wouldn't pay any attention to him and might only make up her mind to see him more."

She frowned. "I realize that. What I was going to suggest was that he might take her with him on his next voyage. And while she was away from the village I would be able to persuade Barnabas Collins to leave here. To go back to London or somewhere else for his own good."

"I doubt if Captain Conrad would consider that," Nathan Forbes said. "Or whether Julia would come on board the ship."

"I know the chances are against it but I wanted to explain to the captain and ask him to consider it." She hesitated. "But you say I will get nowhere with him."

"That's true."

She grimaced wryly. "So it appears I have wasted your time and my own."

"No. There is a chance I may be able to persuade him to consider your suggestion," the mate said slowly. "I won't make any rash promises. But I'll put the proposition to him that it might be good for Julia to see the Indies and have a change of scene. I can try anyway."

"Would you?" Clare looked up at his pleasant face gratefully.

"You have my word, miss," he said, his own cheeks showing crimson. "I don't believe you told me your name."

"I'm sorry," she said. "My name is Duncan. Clare Duncan." She preferred not to mention her title feeling it would be presumptuous.

"Where can I get in touch with you?"

"Barnabas Collins has rented Stormcliff. I am his house guest."

"I see," the young man said. "But I suppose you would prefer that I not call on you there."

She considered quickly. "It wouldn't matter if you came during the day. Would that be all right for you?"

He nodded. "We finish unloading in the morning. Then there'll be a lull of a few days before we begin taking on a mixed cargo of lumber and fish. I'll not be busy until we begin to load."

"So you may be able to give me a report in a few days?"

"I hope so," Nathan Forbes said cautiously. "But you mustn't count too much on it. Captain Conrad is an unhappy, difficult man and not easy to reason with."

"I understand," she said. "And I'm thankful for your advice and for what you're trying to do for me."

Nathan Forbes opened the cabin door for her. "It's best you should go before he gets back. Then there would be no explaining this."

"You're right," she agreed stepping out on deck again. "That would surely wreck any hopes I may have."

He saw her to the wharf, taking her arm to assist her down the rather shaky planks. When she was safely ashore he tipped his cap to her and returned to the *Belle Corliss* and his duties in supervising the unloading.

She stood there for a moment surrounded by the strong sweet odor of molasses again as the men heaved the great casks out of the ship's hold and sent them gently rolling down a plank runway to the wharf. Whenever a cask landed there was a shout from the men on the wharf as they jubilantly caught it and rolled it to the spot where wagons would later pick the casks up. The tall slim masts of the schooner stood starkly against the blue, cloudless sky. Having taken in the picture she turned and walked back up to where she'd tied the brown mare.

She had just gotten up on the seat of the carriage and was about to begin the drive back to Stormcliff when she saw a thin, very erect man in the uniform of a captain walking down the hill in the direction of the *Belle Corliss*. He had the lean face and burning eyes of a fanatic and he looked neither to left nor right. It was a face Clare knew she would not soon forget and she at once decided this must be Captain Will Conrad.

As she began to drive back to the Collins estate she realized how lucky she had been to make a first contact with the young mate of the *Belle Corliss* rather than with her austere captain. She could not imagine that embittered man giving her any kind of hearing. This way she at least had a slight chance. Nearing the end of her journey she passed the plain white cottage where Julia lived. There was no sign of life about the place, although it was hard to see in because of the high barrier of lilac bushes. She continued on to the stable of Collinwood.

The old stableman helped her down from the carriage. "Did Bess give you any bother?" he asked, referring to the mare.

"No," she smiled. "I had a very enjoyable drive."

The old man nodded. And then with a change of mood he glanced darkly toward Stormcliff. "Was that Barnabas over here last night?"

She stared at him in amazement. "I couldn't say. Why do you ask?"

He scowled. "You know he wanders about here at all mad hours."

"I have heard it rumored."

"No rumors," the old man scoffed. "It's a fact. I've seen him myself. Seems to favor the cemetery."

"He's not well," she apologized for him.

"Well enough to cause a heap of trouble," was the stableman's bitter comment. "It's my opinion the man is mad. Wearing that heavy cape all the time and showing himself only after dark. The family did well to go away while he is here. And I don't know what they'll say about that tomb when they get back?"

"What tomb?" she asked with growing consternation.

"One of the real ancient ones," the stableman said disgustedly. "The padlock has been broken off its metal door and someone has been down in there and broken open one of the caskets. The one in which that Josette was buried long ago."

"But why do you think it was Barnabas Collins?"

"He's the only one who'd do such a daft thing," the stableman said in disgust. "Why else has he been wandering out there night after night? And who that was sane would want to look into a box full of dust and bones?"

"Vandals could be responsible," she pointed out. "Thieves looking for any valuables which might have been buried with the remains."

"Not in this town," the old man said with his lip curled in

disgust. "The ones who rob would rather take it from the living than the dead. It had to be him."

"I suppose you could mention it to him," she suggested.

The old man spat on the dry ground. "It would be a waste of time," he said. "He'd only play the great gentleman and deny it. Stare at me with those funny eyes of his and give me that cold English lingo. I don't have any more truck with your Mister Barnabas than I can help. But I'll have a few stories to tell the Collins family when they get back."

"Will that be soon?" she ventured.

"Not soon enough. Maybe a week or two. Meanwhile this daft relative they rented Stormcliff to is frightening the rest of the servants out of their wits. The housekeeper vows he strangled that girl back of the tavern in town. And he very likely is the one who's been terrorizing those other females."

"I think you have the wrong impression of Barnabas Collins," she argued. "He is odd, I'm quite ready to admit that. But I don't consider him dangerous."

The stableman regarded her with squinted eyes. "I wouldn't count too much on that if I were you, miss. You and that pretty maid of yours may be more foolish than wise to remain in that house alone with him and his daft servant."

"I appreciate your concern," she said with a rather chilly dignity. "But I promise you there is no reason for alarm."

She strolled back to Stormcliff feeling much less assured than she had pretended. The stableman's news had added to her growing concern. Barnabas had a dual nature; he had attributes of both the dead and the living. The fragment of the real Barnabas that remained was gentle, considerate and forgiving. But there were moments when the vampire portion of his being took over.

What she continually feared was that one day the vampire would control the whole man. If that should happen Barnabas would be forever lost to her and to all that was important to him. For that reason she had attempted to weigh her love against the forces of evil which were continually trying to destroy him. In spite of her having told Forbes that her romance with Barnabas was over, she knew in her heart this was not completely true. She was still in love with him.

Just one promise that he was going to emerge from his present state would be all she'd need to make her stand steadfastly by him again. Barnabas was wrong. His weird condition did not repel her, but it unnerved her. If she could see just a glimmer of improvement she would soon manage to control her revulsion at the coldness of his touch, the graveyard tone of his skin and the sometimes fetid, bloody smell of his breath. These were unimportant compared to his charm and his gentle soul.

She determined to speak to him and warn him about the talk at Collinwood just as soon as she could. Once again Belle seemed unduly quiet and pale at dinner. Clare suspected that Barnabas had been quenching his diabolical thirst with the girl's blood again. She asked Belle, "Have you been walking with Barnabas these recent evenings?"

The pretty, dark-haired girl regarded her across the table with a distressed expression. "No, my lady."

Clare doubted the conviction in the girl's voice. She said, "You know how dangerous it can be for you."

Belle glanced down at her plate. "Yes," she said in little more than a whisper.

"I cannot always count on what Mister Barnabas tells me," Clare went on. "So I must depend on you to look after yourself."

The girl made another quiet assent but there was no satisfaction for Clare in it. When dinner was ended Clare quickly left the table and went to the kitchen. As she expected, she saw the kitchen door leading to the cellar was unlocked and left ajar. Since sunset was at hand she guessed that Ben was down below rousing his master.

Very softly she descended the stairs and made her way along the black corridor. Far ahead she saw the door of the locked room open and the pale illumination of the candles by Barnabas Collins' coffin showing through it.

As she came up to the doorway she saw Ben raise the cover from the coffin. And after a moment's delay the claw-like hand of Barnabas showed itself on the edge of the coffin, groping for a spot to grip. Once taking hold Barnabas raised himself up from his reclining position and murmured something to Ben. In the next moment he descended from the gray casket and began straightening his coat.

Calling on all her courage Clare made her way into the room. Ben wheeled his stooped figure around in dismay while Barnabas stared at her with cool annoyance.

"You have no right to be down here," he accused her.

Clare regarded him unhappily. "No more right than you had breaking into Josette's tomb last night," she said.

The gaunt, handsome face showed surprise. "How do you happen to know about that?"

"All the servants are talking about it at Collinwood," she said. "And they are sure you're responsible. They think you're mad! And they're just waiting for the Collins family to return to spill out their stories."

Barnabas shrugged. "They are a pack of superstitious fools.

Do you think I haven't dealt with their kind before?"

"The stableman mentioned the girl who was strangled in town," she let him know. "And also the girls who have been attacked lately. He suggested you could be to blame."

Barnabas merely looked resigned. "I'm not nearly as worried about this as you appear to be." He turned to Ben who was standing by, listening. "I don't need you any longer. You may go."

The stooped man bowed. "Yes, sir," he said quietly and left. Now they were alone in the shadowed room together. The candles at the head and foot of the coffin still burned unevenly. Barnabas looked infinitely weary.

"I had to enter Josette's tomb," he told her. "I was searching for something. Something that might have been of help to me. I didn't find it."

"You must keep away from the cemetery in future. They're watching you closely," she warned him.

He smiled crookedly. "Cemeteries are my natural habitat. Even you cannot deny that. There is no law prohibiting my being in a cemetery."

"The Collins cemetery is a private one. Even though you are a member of the family, you have been away a long time. They would certainly resent your breaking down a vault door and despoiling a casket."

"I do not consider my actions amounted to that," Barnabas said. "But I will not argue with you. Have you decided to leave?"

"No."

"You are being foolish, Clare." For a moment he sounded like the considerate Barnabas she had known in London, the Barnabas of charm and sincerity.

"I haven't quite given up yet," she said.

"You should," he warned her. "I have found myself the perfect companion in Julia Conrad. She even reminds me of Josette in many ways. Not physically, so much, but in her manner. After all my years of searching it is quite astonishing."

"It's a liaison you'll regret," Clare warned him. "There is no true love in her. She's never been faithful to any man, including her husband."

"She has made my life bearable," Barnabas told her calmly.

"I have come here making many sacrifices for you!"

He moved his fingers nervously over the silver wolf's head of his walking stick. "You know!" he said in an irritable tone. "That makes all the difference. I will not have pity."

"So you say," she said with a sigh. "But it might be well for you to show some to others. To me and to poor Belle. I'm sure you are going against my pleas and victimizing her."

"What goes on between Belle and myself is our private affair," Barnabas said angrily.

"Not when I'm responsible for her being here," Clare warned him. "If any harm comes to the girl I'll hold you responsible."

Barnabas offered her a mocking bow. "Pray, don't let me detain you any longer, Lady Clare. I have heard enough of your veiled threats and warnings. Do as you please and expect me to do the same."

"Very well," she said, hurt tightening her throat. "But remember what I said about Belle." And with that she walked out of the room and down the long dark corridor to the stairs leading to the kitchen.

CHAPTER 10

She did not see Barnabas again that night. Nor did she see him during the several evenings that followed. Events moved in a routine fashion and she began to wonder if she would ever hear from the young man she'd talked to on the *Belle Corliss*.

It was while she was resting on a bench offering a view of the cliffs and the ocean beyond that he finally came. Almost four days had gone by between their first meeting and his arriving on this warm afternoon. He was riding a spirited black horse which he let cross the even lawn to close to the bench before he dismounted. Holding the bridle in his hand he walked over to her.

She rose from the bench with a smile. "I had just about given you up."

His frank, pleasant face showed good humor. "I was afraid you might. But there was no point in coming until I had some word."

"True," she agreed. And with an eagerness she was unable to conceal she asked, "How have you made out?"

Continuing his hold on the bridle of the restless black horse, he said, "It has gone better than I hoped. I made no mention of your problem. Rather, I suggested that loneliness might be responsible for Julia's reckless behavior. And I've convinced the captain he should take her along when we leave in a week or so."

"How wonderful!" she exclaimed, her heart bounding with excitement at the good news. "Then that should solve everything. With Julia out of the way I'm positive I can manage Barnabas."

The young man looked at her gravely. "Mind you, I'm not promising that Julia will go along with the idea. Or that she won't pretend to cooperate and then back out at the last minute."

"We'll simply hope that doesn't happen," Clare said. "And I don't believe it will."

"How are things at this end?"

"Not good," she said. "Why don't you tie the horse under some shady tree? Then we can talk more easily."

"Not a bad idea," Nathan Forbes agreed. And he led the horse away to a clump of sturdy trees, any one of which would make an ideal hitching post.

Clare sat on the stone bench, again as she waited for him to return. His news, while good, did not mean her scheme would work. Julia could still spoil it all. So could Barnabas, for that matter. She glanced across the lawn and saw the stalwart figure of Nathan Forbes walking back to join her. He had a sailor's rolling stride and there was an immense vitality about him.

Seating himself on the bench beside her he removed his nautical cap so that his curly brown hair was freed to stir idly in the slight ocean breeze.

His serious gray eyes met hers. "I've been asking some questions and finding out things about you," he told her. "For one thing I know it's not plain Clare Duncan but Lady Clare Duncan."

"The title isn't that important," she assured him. "I saw no reason to mention it."

"Could that be because you hoped a mere ignorant sailor like myself would be more interested in helping you if he thought you were closer to his level? Not completely beyond his world?"

Clare blushed. "I can only tell you that I consider you neither behave like nor seem an ignorant sailor to me. I have known many so-called London men of fashion and title who would not measure up to you."

Nathan Forbes smiled. "I like that. Especially since you sound as if you mean it."

"I do."

"Having settled that," he said, "I'll go on to something else. This Barnabas Collins you're so interested in. I've been hearing some weird tales about him."

Clare was at once on the alert. "Really?"

"They say he never shows himself in the day. Is that why you suggested I visit you in the daytime?"

She sighed and stared down at the grass. "That was partly

the reason. I didn't want him to meet you."

"Don't you think it strange he appears only after sunset?"

She shrugged. "He is a scholar. He gives his days to his books."

"And his evenings to strangling poor doxies who become aware that he is not quite normal," Nathan Forbes said calmly. "A girl was found dead behind the tavern the other night and some others have been badly frightened by a mystery man in a cape. The villagers claim Barnabas Collins is the only one around here who wears an Inverness."

Clare looked into the solemn youthful face of the first mate of the *Belle Corliss* and suddenly had the awful feeling that he knew! That the secret of Barnabas Collins was not a secret to him.

Swallowing hard, she said, "You know how these superstitious people can be. They see a phantom behind every tree. And Barnabas is a stranger and odd to them."

Nathan Forbes smiled grimly. "You're suggesting the townsfolk are not used to the ways of London scholars."

"Yes."

"I don't believe Barnabas Collins is a London scholar in the ordinary sense. I've told you I have some knowledge of the history of Collinsport and the Collins family. I've done some research on that score also. Do you know why the first Barnabas left Collinsport?"

She realized there was no stopping him in his revelations now. Quietly she said, "Suppose you tell me."

"I will. Although I don't believe I need to. You're only too well aware of it. Barnabas Collins left Collinsport because of a curse put on him by a jealous girl from the West Indies named Angelique. She turned him into a vampire, one of the living dead. And she condemned him to roam the earth for all time in that state between death and life." He paused dramatically. "So the man you're asking me to help, the man you so plainly love, is that original Barnabas Collins come back to his home. He is a man who normally would be a century or so old in this year 1870. And he is someone who has been tainted with the odor of the grave for more than fifty years."

She sighed. "Do you expect to convince anyone such a wild theory is true?"

"No. Frankly, I don't. But I believe it to be true," he said. "And I think you know it to be so. The local people will settle for the fact he is a madman, a grandson of a man cast out by his family. That is as far as their imaginations will allow them to go."

"Isn't that a good thing?"

"I'm not sure." Nathan Forbes's pleasant face was troubled.

"I suppose you have the romantic idea you can save Barnabas from the curse. But you should remember all that curse entailed. It extended to anyone he loved and who was unfortunate enough to love him. So you should know that any such hopes of helping him are doomed."

"If you can get Julia Conrad away from here he may still be saved," she said.

"I think not," the young mate of the *Belle Corliss* said firmly. "And I'm afraid you may be placing yourself and others in grave danger by clinging to that belief. If Julia is removed from the scene there will be some other obstacle."

"This is not the first time I've heard that," Clare said, recalling the words of the medium aboard the Morning Star. "I still want to do what I can for him. He is so much at the mercy of the fates."

"Say the curse and be frank," Nathan Forbes said grimly. "I'm perhaps the one person in Collinsport to whom you can speak the truth aside from him. Isn't it pity that drives you on now? How can a normal, healthy girl love a dead man?"

She looked at him with worried eyes. "You have been so good and helpful. Don't spoil it with a lot of useless questions now."

"A vampire is here. A threat to the countryside. And you want to protect him with a conspiracy of silence."

"Get Julia away from here and I'll see he leaves Collinsport," she promised.

"Where can he go?" Nathan Forbes demanded. "There is no rest for him anywhere."

"Let me try," she pleaded. "Don't ask for explanations."

"Very well," he said quietly. "I made you a promise and I'll do all I can to live up to it. But I'm not happy about it. Nor am I happy about the danger that exists for you.

"Barnabas wouldn't harm me."

"Not the Barnabas you love," he agreed. "But there is the haunted phantom. You can't predict what dark impulse may drive him to violence."

She couldn't make any reply to this because she knew it was true. She glanced out toward the sea again, her eyes fixed on a graceful square-rigger moving very slowly across the horizon. And it was then without warning that the rugged young first mate of the *Belle Corliss* came close and took her in his arms.

Before she could protest he was pressing her to him. His lips touched hers gently for a long moment before he let her go. His pleasant young face wore a shy expression.

"I suppose I'm going to be hated for doing that," he said.

She touched the fingers of her left hand to her cheek. Staring at him with wonder in her eyes, she asked, "Why did you do it?"

"Because I'm in love with you," he said. "I have been since the moment I first saw you on deck the other day. I know I have no right."

"I don't believe one can be certain of love so quickly," she said, her eyes continuing to search his bronzed young face.

"I have no doubts about my feelings," he assured her. "It is the first time I've so declared myself for any girl."

A sad smile crossed her lovely face. "I find that hard to believe and yet I appreciate your saying it."

He stood up. "It is the truth. I'm only a blunt sailor and no match for the kind of fancy talk a titled lady like yourself is used to hearing."

Clare also rose. "I prefer blunt talk. And please don't continually put so much stress on my title."

"Because of it I know there is no chance for an ordinary man like me," he said. "But there is none could have more respect or feeling for you than myself."

"I believe that," she said. "If things were different I might be glad to hear your declaration."

"You mean he's the one that stands between us," Nathan Forbes said with a frown. "That Barnabas."

"Because of him I'm terribly mixed up as to my future," she admitted.

"By the time the *Belle Corliss* returns you'll be far away from here," he said. "I may never set eyes on you again."

"That doesn't have to be true," she told him. "I have known many stranger things to happen."

"Cold comfort," he said in his blunt way. "Well, I must get back to the ship."

"Will I see you again?"

"You may call on me if you need me," he said, studying her in his serious way. "Otherwise I'll be busy with loading our cargo."

"I"ll remember that," she said with another small smile. "Good luck, Nathan Forbes. You have been my friend."

He nodded without saying anything. Then he turned and went back to where the black horse was tethered. She watched him with a harsh feeling of loneliness. He, at least, loved her. And brief though their acquaintance had been, he had become such a potent force in her life that she found it hard to believe.

He mounted the black horse and as he headed toward the road he waved to her. She waved back and continued to follow him with her eyes as he rode away. With the last glimpse of him her sense of isolation became more compelling than before. The warnings he had voiced about Barnabas only underlined what she had already recognized herself. But she had gone too far in her attempt to help the unfortunate victim of the curse to hesitate now.

With a deep feeling of loss she headed back to the house to dress for dinner. Standing on the front steps was the stooped, sallow-faced Ben. And she realized with some dismay he might have been there for some time. Long enough to have witnessed the romantic scene between herself and Nathan Forbes.

As she met Ben on the steps, she said, "That was the first mate of the *Belle Corliss*. He brought some good news. He believes Captain Conrad may take his wife with him on his voyage to the Indies."

The old man showed no expression. "Indeed, my lady."

"That is what we have wanted," she reminded him. "To get that woman out of the way. Then perhaps we can talk reason to Barnabas."

"I hope so, Lady Duncan," the old man said. "It is often hard to fathom my master."

She gave him a questioning look. "I count on you not to tell him anything that could distress him."

And she went on inside, fairly sure that the old man would keep silent about anything he might have witnessed from the steps. While she knew he feared Barnabas, she also was certain that he wanted to assist her in helping his master.

So she dismissed the episode from her mind. When she went upstairs to dress she was surprised to discover Belle stretched out on the bed in the adjoining room. She went over to the girl and saw that she was not asleep.

"Are you feeling ill?" she asked her.

The dark-haired girl looked up with an expression of bewilderment on her pale features. "I don't know what came over me. I was suddenly dizzy. I had to rest myself."

"No harm done," Clare said at once. She knew what was wrong with the girl. No doubt Barnabas has been feasting himself on her strength nightly. And she was thankful that it would soon be at an end. With Julia away on the *Belle Corliss* she might gain some control over Barnabas.

"Do you want me to help you dress, my lady?" the girl said, raising herself on an elbow.

"No need," Clare said. "I can manage alone nicely. You continue resting."

She changed into a dark gown for the evening and placed a favorite cameo on her bosom. She sat at the big dining room table alone for dinner. Belle did not come down. This was unusual but she decided the girl might benefit more from a sound sleep than the food.

Lonely and worried, she wandered into the big parlor and went over to the pianoforte. It was covered by a light layer of dust and looked as if it had not been played in some time. Sitting down to it she uncovered the keyboard and studied it a moment. Back in London she had played regularly but she'd not touched a piano since she'd begun journeying after Barnabas.

Caressing the keys lightly with her slender fingers she was pleased to discover the piano had a good tone and was not too seriously out of tune. She hesitated and then a remembered theme of Mozart came to her mind and she began to play. Almost at once she became lost in the magic of the music. In the big room with its drawn drapes the shadows of twilight settled rapidly as she went on playing.

She looked up and saw Barnabas standing at the back of the grand piano studying her intently. Her fingers raised from the keys and the melody dissipated in midair. She stared at him in shy confusion.

On his gaunt, handsome face there was an expression of ineffable sadness. He straightened his caped shoulders and in a quiet voice said, "That was lovely, Clare."

"I didn't realize you had come in."

"It takes me back to London. Your drawing room and the many times you played for me then." He sighed. "I wish we could recapture those days."

She rose from the piano bench. "Why shouldn't we?"

He shook his head. "Too late. In any case I hear you have found yourself a sailor."

She froze where she stood. So Ben had talked to Barnabas. She said tautly, "Don't place too much weight on that."

His eyes studied her with deep melancholy. "I think it is good. You should forget me. Let me amuse myself as I must. You must find your own happiness."

"My happiness is with you," she said.

"That was so," he said. "It's not true any longer. Since you came to join me here I have brought you only misery. Admit it."

"That doesn't have to be."

"Hold on to your sailor, Clare," Barnabas told her. "He offers your best hope of happiness." And without waiting for her reply, he left the shadowed room.

She stared after him in a turmoil of emotions. In spite of all she could do she felt that he was moving further and further away from her. She was losing him! If Julia eased even temporarily the memories which haunted him perhaps that was all that could be hoped for. It was possible she was wrong in trying to interfere, to save the love which had once existed between her and Barnabas but which now seemed cold and remote.

Was she more interested in her own happiness than his? She hoped this was not so. She had crossed the Atlantic to be with him in the hope of salvaging him in some fashion. Once the curse was broken he could return to a normal life. And she had never given up thinking that this could one day happen. Yet never had it seemed so unlikely.

There was the matter of Belle. She had determined to upbraid him about his treatment of the attractive maid. But he had gone before she'd had the opportunity. And would he have listened to her in any case? Were the impulses driving him under the shadow of the curse stronger than he could manage? If so, her words would only fall on deaf ears. Barnabas might regret the ill he was doing Belle and still be unable to desist.

It was a dreadful dilemma. And she began to doubt that even with Julia away she could do anything to change the Devil's pattern into which the curse had plunged this man she loved. Darkness came and she wandered through the empty silence of the great stone house like a lost soul. At last she decided to go up to bed. Before retiring she looked in on Belle and was relieved to find her sleeping.

The weird melancholy call of a night bird woke her up. She had no idea how long she'd been asleep. Her room was in pitch darkness and all at once she had the conviction the cry she'd heard had been some kind of warning. The premonition of danger pressed thickly around her as she sat up staring wide-eyed into the shadows.

And then she thought of Belle. A strong feeling of concern for the girl surged through her. She became so uneasy that she groped in the darkness for her dressing gown and slipping it on, made her way across the room to the door leading to the maid's bedchamber.

Softly opening the door, she crossed to Belle's bedside. The covers were thrown back and the bed was empty. A small cry of dismay passed her lips. And without hesitation she rushed out of the room and into the corridor. There was still no sign of the missing girl. She made her way down the stairs and knew further despair when she saw the entrance door was open.

So Belle was somewhere out in the night! With no thought of herself she went out and down the steps. Because of the lack of moon or stars the visibility was limited. She slowly made her way across the lawn, straining for some glimpse of the sleepwalking Belle. Within a short time she was so close to the cliffs that the roar of the breakers came loud and frightening.

She hesitated as the eerie combination of darkness and

beating waves caused her flesh to crawl. And then in the distance she saw Belle walking unsteadily along the cliff's edge.

She cried out, "Belle!"

But the maid walked on as if she hadn't heard her. A moment later before her terrified eyes the girl suddenly stumbled and quickly vanished. Clare screamed again and rushed forward to the spot where she'd last seen the unfortunate Belle. When she reached it there was no sign of the girl.

Panting from fear and effort she braced herself to peer down over the dizzy height of the cliff. There was only darkness below and the pound of the sea. With another scream she wheeled around and raced back to the house.

She found Ben and Barnabas waiting for her on the steps. Barnabas came to meet her with concern on his handsome face. "What is wrong?" he demanded. "What are you doing out here at this hour?"

"Belle!" she cried hysterically. "I'm sure she's gone over the cliff!"

Barnabas grasped her by the arms and stared at her with his burning eyes. "What mad talk is this?"

"It's true," she insisted through her sobs. "I watched it happen just now. It's your fault!"

He frowned, still grasping her. "My fault?"

"I warned you that you were sapping her strength, taking away her desire to live. But you wouldn't listen to me! Now she is dead and you have lost a victim to prey on!"

Sheer horror showed on the gaunt, handsome face. "No!" he said harshly. Releasing her, he rushed off in the darkness in the direction of the cliff. The stooped Ben followed him with a faltering gait.

Clare remained there on the steps waiting. Neither the cool night nor the passage of time made any difference to her. She was numbed to all save the tragedy which she had witnessed. And when she saw the forms of Ben and Barnabas come toward her out of the shadows and Barnabas was holding the limp body of Belle in his arms she was not even surprised. She had known it would end this way.

Barnabas came to stand mutely before her with Belle's broken body held close to him. The look on his gaunt, handsome face was tortured beyond anything she had known before. Ben stood stricken at his master's side. Without a word Barnabas mounted the steps and brushed by her. Ben followed him. She remained there, still stunned.

Later, when she went inside, she found Belle's body carefully placed on a chaise longue in the drawing room. Ben stood silently by as an attendant and mourner. But Barnabas was nowhere in sight.

Ben approached her. "I'm sorry, my lady. What can I do to help?"

Belle's funeral was held in the midday sunshine. She was buried in the private cemetery of the Collins family. Clare had not been able to secure the permission of the Collins family since they were still away. But the clergyman in Collinsport pointed out that a section of the burial ground had been reserved for servants of the family and he had no doubt that it would be all right to bury the lovely Belle there.

Nathan Forbes stood by Clare's side as the plain wooden coffin was lowered into the freshly dug grave. And as Clare watched with tears in her eyes a grim determination came into her mind. For the good of all, including Barnabas himself, he must be destroyed. His depredations must be brought to an end. The memory of the final destruction of Dr. Henri Fontaine was clear in her mind. She knew what must be done!

CHAPTER 11

The funeral was over. Nathan Forbes and Clare strolled together silently along the very cliff where Belle had plunged to her death. She felt the man at her side must be having many of the same thoughts as herself. So when they came to the bench on the main estate of Collinwood, she paused to sit down and stare out at the ocean. The young ship's officer sat beside her.

After a moment, she asked, "Has it been arranged? Is Julia going to sail aboard the *Belle Corliss*?"

"Yes," he said. "It's all settled. I understand there was a deal of argument between Captain Will and his wife. But she is going."

"I'm afraid I now feel that won't be enough," she said, giving him a solemn glance.

Nathan Forbes's pleasant face reflected her own grave mood. "I think I understand what you mean."

"He must be done away with, Nathan," she said. "For his own good."

"Is that possible?"

She nodded. "I helped finish another such unfortunate, Dr. Fonatine on the island of Mont St. Michel. It requires a stake of hawthorn through the heart."

"You're sure of your feelings in this regard?" the young man at her side asked. "Your talk is quite different now from the other day."

"Events have made me see things in a truer light," she said quietly. "I'm resigned to the fact there is no longer hope for Barnabas and me."

"Does that mean there could be hope for us?"

Her eyes fixed on the shimmering silver of the ocean again. "There will be plenty of time to find that out. Just now the problem is Barnabas. Are you willing to help me?"

"I will do what I can."

She kept her eyes on the ocean not wanting to look at him while she continued. "First, you must get the required items. A hawthorn stake with a sharp point and a mallet with which to drive it through the heart of Barnabas. I cannot help you. I would feel like a traitor, though I know it must be done. But I can tell you where and when to find him. Every evening at sunset Ben descends to the cellar and unlocks the door of the room where Barnabas rests in his coffin during the daylight hours."

"And I'm to follow Ben down there and settle it in that room," the man at her side said.

"Yes. I think that would be the easiest and best way. You'll get no opposition from Ben. He is old and weak and I doubt if he'll interfere with you in any case. He is as alarmed about what is going on with Barnabas as the rest of us."

"It will have to be soon," Nathan Forbes reminded her. "We sail in three days."

"Can you be ready tomorrow at sunset?"

"Yes."

"Then let us make that the time," she suggested. "In case anything goes wrong you will have another chance the following night."

"I'll be here," he promised.

She turned to him with an agitated expression on her pretty face. "You must be careful! Barnabas can be wily! And he is desperately strong! Once you make the attack on him you dare not falter."

The young man's face was grim. "I know all that."

Reaching out a slender hand to touch one of his, she said, "I have no right to ask this of you. It is a kind of murder. But there is no other way."

"I'm willing to risk it," he said. "I'd risk a lot more for a chance to marry you."

And he took her in his arms for another warm embrace. His kiss was the ardent one of a lover. She surrendered to him with the consoling knowledge that she was in the arms of a man ready to take any risk for her. And for perhaps the first time she knew there was more than mere friendship in her feelings toward him.

Releasing her, he said, "I'll be here around six. And I'll wait by the barns for your signal to enter the house."

"I'll come out to you after Ben has gone downstairs," she said.

"It shouldn't be difficult," he reassured her. "Barnabas won't be expecting anything like this."

"I hope not," she worried.

But Barnabas had an incredible way of finding out secrets. All that night and the following day she was haunted by the fear she might be sending Nathan Forbes into a trap. Yet it was a chance which had to be taken. The great stone house seemed more ghostly than ever with Belle gone. Ben moved about silently like a pale apparition. And Barnabas carefully avoided her.

The afternoon of the next day was marked by the fog drifting in. The bright weather came to a damp, dismal end as the heavy rolling fog circled the house and settled its wet hand on everything. For most of the day she remained in her bedroom. Once when she went to the window she was surprised to discover that she couldn't even see Collinwood, although the main house was only a short distance away.

As evening approached the fog became even heavier. And the melancholy blast of the foghorn from Collins Point was a constant reminder of the change in the weather. Clare dressed for dinner and went downstairs just before the time when day ended. She went into the library on the pretense of searching for a book since it gave her a listening post to know when Ben unlocked the door leading to the cellar and went down below.

Her nerves were so on edge that she didn't even read the titles of the books she picked at random from the shelves. She pretended to glance through them as she waited for the familiar sounds that would tell her Ben had gone down to minister to his master.

They finally came. She heard the key turn in the lock and then the door creaked open and Ben start down the stone steps. Losing not a minute, she hurried from the library and out of the house. When she reached the barns she had a dreadful moment when it seemed that Nathan Forbes had not come as he'd promised. But as she stared toward the fog-shrouded barns he suddenly appeared.

Running to meet him, she said, "Now!"

He was carrying a rough sack in which she supposed he had the stake and mallet. He nodded and without a word hurried by her toward the house. She followed but somehow couldn't bring herself to go inside. She'd luckily worn a shawl for protection and now she stood by the stone house clutching it around her against the damp and cold.

The wait seemed interminable. And when at last Nathan Forbes emerged hastily from the rear door of the big house she at once sensed something had gone wrong. But at least he was alive and unharmed. She met him halfway across the yard.

"He fooled us!" the young first mate said unhappily, glancing back at the house.

"How?"

"When I entered the cellar it was in complete darkness," he said. "The candles you spoke of as being on the coffin had been snuffed out. I took out the stake and mallet and moved forward. As my eyes grew accustomed to the dark I made out the shadow of Barnabas. I recognized the outline of his cape. I knocked him out with the mallet; then I drove the stake between his shoulder blades. When it was done I struck a light to make sure of what I'd accomplished. It wasn't Barnabas. It was Ben!"

"Oh, no!" she gasped.

Nathan Forbes nodded grimly. "He'd found out somehow and made Ben put on the Inverness, knowing I'd be misled by it in the darkness."

"So he's somewhere in there!"

"Or out here in the fog stalking us," the young man said, his arm around her protectively. "It's hard to say what he'll do now."

Clare shut her eyes. "And Ben's body is still in the cellar."

"I left it where it was," he admitted. "I was shocked to find I'd killed the wrong man. I'm a murderer!"

She opened her eyes and looked up at him forlornly. "You can't be blamed for his murder! You didn't intend to kill him. It was Barnabas you were trying to rid us of. And Barnabas tricked us!"

Nathan Forbes's eyes were fixed on the stone house. Gripping her by the arm, he said, "Look! The house is on fire!"

And he was right. She could see the flames through the rear windows. Already the fire seemed to have gained a good start. She stared at the flames in dismay, knowing that the fire would quickly bring the servants from Collinwood. And then they would find Ben's body.

"How can it have started?"

"For it to get this headway it must have been set," Nathan Forbes declared grimly. "He's done it."

"Why?"

"His own reasons, whatever they may be," the young man said grimly. "In a few minutes the flames will be bursting through the roof. He's set it on the top and lower floors. He wasn't taking any chances of failure."

Nathan was right. The smoke began to curl from under the roof's eaves and then the fire burst through the roof itself. Long tongues of yellow flame shot upward. The house was becoming an inferno. She and Nathan stood back a distance transfixed. They were still standing there when the first of the workers from Collinwood arrived. There was much shouting and attempts to combat the fire and salvage some of the furnishings. But it was hopeless. Stormcliff was doomed!

The darkness of the night was dispelled by the blazing illumination from the burning house. She and Nathan Forbes had fallen back a distance from the noisy crowd of servants and townspeople who had gathered to watch the spectacle. It was while they were standing on the outer fringe of the crowd that she turned her eyes from the fire to see Barnabas Collins in his familiar cape and carrying his cane, stationed a few feet away regarding them with a cold calmness.

She broke away from Nathan Forbes and advanced to him. "Why did you do it?" she demanded.

He arched a heavy black brow. "Destroy Stormcliff? It seemed the best possible way to cover up your gentleman friend's crime. He murdered poor Ben, you know."

"Because he thought Ben was you!" Clare said brokenly.

Barnabas nodded. "I was well aware of your plot. I'm not as easy to be rid of as Henri Fontaine. But I have returned good for evil. I have covered up the crime. When they find Ben's skeleton in the burning rubble they'll think he died in the fire. So now I'll strike a bargain with you two."

Nathan Forbes had advanced to Clare's side. "We'll make no deals with you, Barnabas."

"You had better," Barnabas said with meaning. "My silence for yours. I'm planning to take passage on the *Belle Corliss* for the Indies. I know you hoped to part Julia and me by having her husband take her on the voyage. Well, I plan to go as well. I have heard of a witch doctor in Barbados who has helped cases of my sort. I want to seek his help."

Clare stared at him. "I wonder if that's so. Or if you're merely using it as an excuse to be with her."

"I could persuade Julia not to take the trip if that was what I wanted," Barnabas pointed out. "I must make this journey to Barbados."

Nathan Forbes said, "How do you know Captain Conrad will accept you as a passenger?"

"It has already been arranged," Barnabas told him.

"And you really do intend to seek help down there?" Clare asked.

"I give you my word," Barnabas told her. "Do you think I want to go on forever like this?"

She exchanged glances with Nathan Forbes. Then she said, "I'll take your word you are in earnest and not merely doing this to be with Julia on one condition."

The man in the Inverness coat raised his eyebrows. "What is your condition?"

"That I shall also be a passenger on the *Belle Corliss*. So that I may be there when you consult this doctor. After all, I have a deep interest."

"Indeed you do," Barnabas said in his mocking fashion. "Even though you have chosen to give your heart to this young man."

"Let's have no discussion of that," Nathan Forbes broke in angrily.

"My pardon," Barnabas bowed. And to Clare, he said, "I see no reason why there should be any difficulty in persuading Captain Conrad to take you along as well."

The young first mate turned to her. "I'm not sure it's wise, Clare. It's a long voyage. A lot could happen on the way."

"No, I want to go," she insisted. "I want to visit this voodoo doctor when Barnabas consults him."

Nathan Forbes gave her a troubled look. "I don't like it."

"From the beginning I've been motivated by a wish to see Barnabas freed from his curse," she reminded the young man. "Do not expect me to lose interest now." She turned to address Barnabas again, but he had vanished!

The *Belle Corliss* set sail for Barbados two days later with Captain Will Conrad's wife Julia aboard and two passengers, Barnabas Collins and Clare. It was a dark gloomy evening when they left Collinsport harbor for the heaving coastal waters. The crew of eleven men worked hard on the last minute preparations. And they also toiled to raise the canvas on the trim little schooner as she headed out to sea.

Barnabas still kept aloof from Clare. And in the first hours aboard he spent a good part of his time on deck talking with Julia Conrad. They took a position near the bow of the schooner while Clare stayed aft. The ship was loaded down with lumber and a small amount of general cargo. Clare's quarters were in the aft cabins along with those of the officers and other passengers. The crew lived forward where the galley was also located.

Nathan Forbes took over the captain's duties as the ship set sail. He stood at the elbow of the helmsman until they were well on course. Then he joined Clare at the railing near the stern.

Clare smiled wanly. "We're underway," she said.

He nodded. "And I see that Barnabas is losing no time in joining his lady love," he said. "He'd better be careful. The captain is in one of his bad moods. It could lead to trouble. The captain is very jealous of Julia, even though he realizes the kind of woman she is."

"He's not being very discreet," she agreed. "We can only hope he'll use more judgment as the voyage goes on. But he is going to be dependent on her. Where else can he get the blood he requires to sustain him?"

Nathan Forbes frowned. "Just so long as he doesn't bother you."

"He has never once tried that," she said. "But poor Belle was his willing victim until it cost her her life." She steadied herself against the rocking of the schooner on the rougher waters. And she noticed the lifeboat carried on davits rigged across the stem. "Is that where you always carry the lifeboat?" she asked.

"Yes," he said. "Because of the swinging booms and sails we keep a clear deck as much as possible. There is another boat on the port side by the rear cabins. But it's a good deal smaller."

Clare glanced up at the dark clouded skies. "Could beginning a voyage in this weather be an omen?"

"I hope not," he said. "According to the glass it's due to clear. I'm more worried about the danger of storms brewing aboard than on the sea."

And Clare knew that in a very real way he was right. At dinner Julia flirted outrageously with Barnabas in spite of glowering glances from her reticent, brooding husband. Barnabas gave all his attention to the pretty wife of the captain, largely ignoring everyone else.

Clare and Nathan Forbes talked at the table but were unable to draw Captain Conrad into the conversation. He sat glaring sullenly at his wife and Barnabas as they laughed and conversed as if they were the only ones present.

On the second day out the weather changed. The sea became calm and the Gulf Stream made it unusually warm. With all sails raised the *Belle Corliss* majestically nosed toward the Indies. Except for the tensions aboard all was well. Barnabas remained in the cabin assigned to him during the day so that helped.

But again in the evening he gave his time and attention to entertaining Julia. Before Clare turned in for the night she spotted them far to the bow along the rail. The moonlight plainly revealing the arm of Barnabas around the captain's errant wife. She knew that Barnabas had a double motive. He required the rash beauty's blood along with her affection.

The question was, how long would Captain Will Conrad

stand for their behavior? Clare believed that Barnabas had no intention of consulting a voodoo doctor. She was becoming more and more certain that he had made the passage merely to be with the beauty who had caught him up in her spell.

The following day she talked earnestly to Nathan Forbes about the possibility of discussing Barnabas Collins with the captain. "If Captain Conrad realized that Barnabas is a doomed and desperate man, one of the living dead, perhaps he would look on his actions with his wife in a different light."

"It's a sound thought," the young man agreed as they stood together amidships. "But the captain is in no mood to be talked to rationally. He's barely left his quarters all day. He's been pouring down rum in a fashion I've never known him to before."

Clare stared at him in consternation. "Then surely we can't avoid trouble."

"Unless you are able to warn Julia and reason with her."

"I can try," she worried. "She only jeered at me before."

That afternoon she had an ideal chance to talk to the captain's wife. She met her in the stern of the ship, studying the trailing foam in its wake. The sullen beauty was staring at the sea raptly and Clare had an excellent chance to observe her neck. The marks of Barnabas were plainly upon it.

Moving close to Julia she said, "May I give you some advice?"

Julia looked at her in arrogant surprise. "I think we understand each other. I have nothing to discuss with you."

"Be careful with Barnabas," she warned her. "He doesn't seem to care what trouble he causes with your husband."

"My husband is a fool!" Julia sneered. "And Barnabas has promised we shall leave the ship in the Indies and live there together."

"Barnabas can offer you nothing but misery!" Clare argued. "He is one of the living dead. A vampire! Do you know what that means?"

Julia shook head. "I don't believe you. Barnabas warned me you would tell me some wild story."

"But it's true!"

"I'll give you more truth," Julia said angrily. "You are in love with Barnabas and jealous because I have taken him from you."

"I did love him once. Now I only pity and fear him," Clare declared. "You do not know the danger you have thrust yourself into."

"And I do not want to talk to you any more about it!" Julia turned her back on her.

So it was hopeless. Even the crew noticed what was taking

place. Nathan Forbes had told Clare there was much gossip going on in the forecastle. At dinner that night Captain Conrad did not make an appearance. Barnabas and Julia paid no attention to this, carrying on as happily as before. But Clare was in a state of panic.

The storm of passions burst forth at twilight. Barnabas and Julia were together on the forward deck. It happened that Clare and Forbes were standing near the helmsman in the stem. Suddenly Captain Conrad came staggering out of his quarters with a pistol in his hand and unevenly made his way toward the two.

Crew members lolling amidships were at once alerted to the drama that was taking place. They stared in consternation at the progress of the drunken captain toward his wife and Barnabas. The first to react was Nathan Forbes, who uttered an oath and rushed after the skipper.

But it was too late. Captain Conrad lifted the pistol and fired point-blank at Barnabas. Julia screamed and threw herself in front of the gaunt, handsome man, taking the full force of the first bullet. She slumped to the deck as her husband fired at Barnabas again.

Barnabas showed no reaction to the bullet that had surely pierced him in a vital place. He swiftly lifted his black cane and drew from it a vicious looking slim sword which he plunged into the captain, sending him staggering back, arms upstretched. The pistol fell from the captain's hand and he fell back on the deck.

Barnabas dropped the sword and bent over the outstretched form of Julia. By this time Nathan Forbes had reached the scene and was doing what he could for Captain Conrad. The crew had recovered from the shock which had left them stunned for a moment. Now they surged forward with cries of rage and consternation.

Clare pushed her way through the cluster of watching crewmen and joined Nathan Forbes, who was kneeling by his captain. Now he looked up at her. "He's dead."

She turned to the other side of the deck where Barnabas had lifted Julia in his arms. His handsome face was contorted by anguish. "Help me with her," he begged Clare. "She's still alive."

Clare said nothing, but followed him down amidships and to the cabins aft. The crew parted to let them through, the shock of what they'd seen still showing on their faces. Barnabas marched directly to the captain's quarters and set Julia gently down on the bunk there. She was deathly pale and her dress front was stained with blood.

"Can't someone do something?" he begged Clare.

"I'll get Mr. Forbes," she said. "He's best qualified for any surgery she may need."

Nathan Forbes came and labored feverishly over the

wounded girl. He recovered the bullet, but her breathing was dangerously shallow and her heartbeat grew weaker all the time. Barnabas paced up and down the rear deck as he waited for reports on her condition.

He was standing by the railing staring up at the stars when Clare finally came out to tell him the captain's wife was dead. Barnabas looked white and stricken. He stared at her blankly.

"What shall I do now?" he asked her in a hoarse whisper.

"You were wrong," Clare accused him. "You caused her death just as you caused Belle's. You didn't actually kill either of them, but you brought about the conditions that caused their deaths."

"I meant them no harm," he said in the safe low tone. "Julia was my salvation. She wouldn't even listen to the truth about me."

"It was a false escape," Clare said. "My love for you was stronger. I could face your tragedy. She couldn't."

He studied her sadly. "I've lost you," he said. "Be honest. You are in love with Forbes."

"That came afterward."

"It would have happened," he told her. "Now I am completely alone."

"What about the voodoo doctor in Barbados?" she said. "You can still see if he can help you."

"I'll never reach Barbados," he said brokenly and turned away from her, his caped shoulders outlined against the starry sky.

Barnabas retreated to his cabin at dawn as usual. Nathan Forbes presided over a funeral service for the captain and the body was sent over the side as was the custom. Julia's dead body still rested on the bunk in the captain's quarters.

Forbes came to Clare with a worried look after the funeral service. "The crew are in a bad state," he confided to her. "They don't understand what has gone on. They saw the captain fire a bullet directly into the heart of Barnabas Collins and he's still alive. The forecastle is full of rumors of evil spirits and a curse on the ship."

She gazed at him in panic. "What can happen?"

"They could mutiny. The captain has been killed. It's a question of how long I can keep them in line. I don't fear violence from them as much as I'm afraid of desertion."

"Then what?"

"I'd somehow have to bring the ship into port alone with the small help you and Barnabas can offer me. We're off the Carolina coast, almost within sight of the shore. If anything happens, I hope it happens soon."

"I'm wondering about Barnabas," she said.

"What about him?"

"How long will he be able to stand his thirst for blood with Julia gone? There's only me left."

The young first mate looked grim. "He'd better manage. The first thing he has to do is answer to a court for his part in what happened last night."

"I doubt if you can get him to," she said. "He'll disappear."

"I've thought of that," he admitted. "But my worst worry is the crew."

And Clare knew his worry was well founded. The seamen went about their tasks with a sullen reluctance and scowls for her and the first mate. When Barnabas appeared at sunset they included him in their angry stares. Barnabas in his Inverness and carrying his silver-headed cane seemed not to even see them. His handsome face looked to have withered and aged.

Later he went into the captain's quarters and to her horror came out again with the body of the dead Julia in his arms. Looking neither to right nor left he walked to the bow of the ship and stood at the most extreme point with the body held outstretched over the sea. After a moment he released it to drop into the churning water.

Nathan Forbes went angrily to reprimand him but by the time he drew near, Barnabas had vanished. It was as simple as that. One moment he was standing there, the next he was gone. This was not lost on the watching crew. And Clare waiting in the background could hear their troubled murmuring.

CHAPTER 12

The bell had sounded the half-hour after nine as the tension torn schooner drifted idly in a calm sea off the coast of Carolina. Elijah, the West Indian crew member most trusted by Nathan Forbes, was doing his turn at the wheel. There was a moon, at times obscured by dark clouds. Nathan and Clare joined the helmsman on deck as Nathan was anxious to query him about the attitude of the crew.

"What are they saying in the forecastle?" he asked the big man.

Elijah's face was an expressionless mask. The big man did not look at Nathan but kept staring ahead. "It's plenty bad, boss," he said in his deep bass voice.

"You mean there's a chance of trouble?"

The big man's eyes rolled so that the whites of them were plainly visible. "The crew's talkin' about the voodoo, boss. They think that Barnabas is a zombie or maybe a vampire. Anyhow, bullets don't do him no harm!"

Nathan frowned. "That's ridiculous talk. The bullet must have missed him."

"No, boss," the big man was emphatic. "Elijah saw with his own eyes. The bullet went into him all right. And it did him no harm. He is one of the Devil's own."

"You're mistaken," Nathan argued somewhat weakly. Clare

felt she should speak up. "Even if what you say is true, Elijah, Barnabas can't harm you."

The big man glanced at her with fear shining in his eyes. "He brings a curse to everyone on board. The *Belle Corliss* will be cursed!"

"We'll make the nearest port as soon as we get a breeze for our sails," Nathan told the big man. "And then you'll see how much of a zombie or vampire Barnabas Collins is. He'll be taken before a court for the captain's murder."

"That man never will see a court," Elijah predicted. "He can come and go as he likes."

They left Elijah and walked over to the port rail where they could talk with some degree of privacy. She thought Nathan looked dreadfully weary. The strain of the previous night's tragedy had taken its toll from the young man.

He frowned. "You heard him. It's impossible to reason with those fellows."

"They've been brought up with superstition," she said. "So maybe they're more alert to the dangers we face than we are."

"It'll only take a single spark to send them into rebellion," he worried. "From now on we can't be too careful. I wonder where Barnabas has hidden himself."

"Perhaps it's as well he remains hidden," she suggested. "The very sight of him terrifies the crew now."

"There's that side to it," Nathan agreed. He gazed at her worriedly. "I wouldn't feel so nervous if I had only myself to think about. But I have to somehow protect you."

"I'll manage," she assured him with a false calmness. She didn't dare to let him realize how terrified she actually was.

"You're caught between dangers," he reminded her. "From the crew and from Barnabas."

"I can blame no one but myself," she said. "I insisted on making the trip. I didn't guess then that the Captain and Julia would be dead before we had even gone half way."

"Nor did I," he said. "Though I was against your coming. But you wanted to help Barnabas."

"I still say he's more to be pitied than censored," she told him. "It was Julia who wantonly led him on. And the captain did shoot his wife and him before he attacked him with the sword."

Nathan Forbes smiled grimly. "Next you'll be saying that Barnabas should be completely forgiven since he is the victim of that ancient curse, is not responsible."

"Isn't it true?"

"It well may be," he said in a tense voice. "But I only wish I had that hawthorn stake with me. I'd soon try to plunge it into his heart and end this nightmare."

"Not while there's still a chance he may be saved," she pleaded.

"You really believe that?"

"He spoke of that witch doctor in Barbados. They have powerful voodoo in the islands. I have heard strange stories of the miraculous cures they've managed. Why shouldn't Barnabas be one of them?"

The young man shook his head. "I don't believe in any of that. I say there is only one cure for those like Barnabas Collins. They must be put to rest for all time."

"Will you really head for the nearest port when the wind comes up?"

"Yes. It's the proper thing to do."

"Let's hope the crew will cooperate until then," she said.

He glanced up at the cloudy sky. "The barometer is dropping. I don't like the prospects of the weather. This unnatural calm could be the forerunner to something really bad."

Clare shivered. "We have problems enough without a storm."

"It could pass," he said. "Meanwhile, you'd better get some rest. I'll see you to your cabin."

"I'd say there was a small chance I'll sleep," she warned him. "Too much has happened."

But he saw her to the door and kissed her goodnight. As she stepped inside he started back for the deck. She had no sooner closed the door of the tiny cabin when she was seized from behind and a clammy, cold hand pressed hard over her mouth making it impossible to scream for help. She fought viciously to free herself but it was no use.

Barnabas spoke softly in her ear. "Promise me not to cry out or try to get away and I'll let you go."

Clare considered quickly. There was nothing she could do but accept his terms. He was much too strong for her. So she managed a weak nod to let him know she agreed.

At once he released her. The glow of the single tallow candle in the cabin highlighted his gaunt, handsome face. He seemed tense and older than she had ever seen him look before. He had come a long way from being the fashionable man-about-town in London.

He said, "Do you know I'm slowly dying for want of blood?"

"You should have thought of that earlier while Julia was still alive," she told him. "You knew how dependent you were on her."

His burning eyes fixed on her throat. "I have only to kiss your throat and my agony would be over. You wouldn't remember anything about it. It would be a kind of dream experience for you."

"I understand too well," she said scornfully. "I saw Belle too many times after you had feasted on her. The only way you can have my blood is to take it from me by force."

"You pity me and that is bitter enough," he said. "Your blood would taste like vinegar to me!"

"So you will perish from the lack of it!"

Barnabas gazed at her in disbelief. "You loved me once. How can you so soon hate me?"

She continued to regard him with that scornful look. "You were right the first time. I do not hate you. I pity you. It's the curse we're fighting, not you."

"Inseparable," he said with weary resignation. "This time I'm still in command of my soul. But don't count on being so lucky again." He turned with his broad shoulders slumped wearily under the cape and left the cabin.

Her heart was still pounding from fear. She knew how close it had been. How long Barnabas could keep the full evil of his darker side in check? When he became truly desperate for the female blood which he must have to live, she would face the ultimate danger.

As she'd told Nathan Forbes, sleep was out of the question. She tossed on the hard mattress of her bunk, remaining fully clothed since she had no idea how soon an emergency might arise. The *Belle Corliss* had become a ship of terror.

She must have dozed off briefly, for she opened her eyes with a start at the sound of a heavy pounding on her cabin door. As she roused herself she heard a familiar voice cry out.

"Clare! Wake up!" It was Nathan.

She opened the door and saw the look of desperation on his pleasant face. "What is it now?"

"The crew! They've deserted the ship! All of them!"

"They couldn't have!"

"Come on deck and see for yourself," he told her. And he took her by the arm and led her out onto the darkness of the deck. Pointing to the stern he said, "They took the big lifeboat. You can see she's gone."

She stared through the shadows and saw that it was. Then she turned a startled gaze to the young man. "But why?"

"They're convinced the ship is cursed and Barnabas is some kind of a dead man."

"What happens now?"

"I don't know," he confessed. "I can't manage a ship this size alone. And if a storm comes up she'll founder."

She stared out at the ocean. "Maybe they'll change their minds and come back."

"That's not likely," he said dryly.

"So there's just the three of us left aboard."

He nodded grimly. "You, I and Barnabas. And it's only a question of time before he attacks."

Her face showed fear. "I can't believe that."

"When the thirst for blood reaches its peak he'll have no choice."

"Another ship may come by. We could signal for help."

Nathan Forbes shook his head and then stared out at the ocean. "We're only a mile or at the most two from the coast of Carolina," he said. "I'd say we could make it easily in the small boat if the storm doesn't come up too soon."

"You'd leave the *Belle Corliss*?" she exclaimed in surprise. "She's your ship now. Your responsibility."

"I have a greater responsibility to you," he said evenly. "Go get whatever few things you want to take with you. I'll round up some provisions and water. Then we're taking off in the small boat."

Her eyes were wide. "And leave Barnabas here to slowly die?"

"It's as good a way as a stake through his heart," Nathan said brusquely. "I haven't time to worry about him. I'm too concerned about you."

She saw there was to be no arguing with him. So she hurried to her cabin and gathered her few personal belongings. She picked up a warm shawl which she hoped might offer some protection in the small boat. Then she went out on deck again to meet Nathan. He had rounded up packages of food and a keg of fresh water. "We could miss direction or be caught by a current and not make the shore."

The launching of the small boat turned out to be a complicated business. It took all the effort of which she and Nathan were capable. All during this time of stress there was no sign of Barnabas. At last they were in the lifeboat and casting off from the schooner. Clare was still thinking about Barnabas alone on the ship. She tried to peer back through the darkness and for just a fleeting moment thought she saw him standing by the rail watching them leave. Then he vanished.

She turned to Nathan who was already straining at the oars. "Should we have left him there?"

"Let him use his supernatural powers," Nathan said grimly. "Our safety rests on my calloused hands at the moment."

He had not exaggerated. With the coming of dawn there was still no sign of the shore. Nor was the *Belle Corliss* in sight. The small boat was billowed by great waves and Nathan's efforts at the oars seemed to count for nothing. Clare began to worry that they would have been better off to have remained on the schooner.

With the rising of the sun the blazing heat became merciless and there was no shelter from it. By noon they were glistening with perspiration and parched. Nathan grudgingly ladled out the fresh water, warning her that the good supply they had would not last long enough if they were unfortunate enough to be carried away from the shore.

She tried to see some sign of land but the waves extended endlessly. "Do you think we are headed the right way?"

"Unless my compass lies."

"But surely land ought to be in sight by now."

He worked stolidly at the oars, stripped to the waist now. His powerful bronzed body gleaming with the sweat of his labors and the heat. "I may have made a mistake in the distance. We could have been further from the coast than I reckoned."

"Surely some coastal craft will come along and see us," she worried.

"We can hope so," he said.

But none came. The day wore on and soon they were faced with another night on the ocean in the small boat. Clare was beginning to lose hope that they would ever sight land but she dared not voice her fears to Nathan Forbes. He was as resolute and helpful as she could wish. And with the darkness came relief from the sun and a cooling air for which she was grateful.

When they had finished their Spartan evening meal, Nathan said, "Maybe when dawn comes we'll sight land."

"Do you think so?" she asked eagerly.

"I'd expect to. Even if we were further from shore than I thought when we started out."

"What could have happened to the longboat with the crew?"

He shook his head. "I don't know."

"Do you think they'll make land?"

"Their chances are better than ours," he said frankly. "They have more men and a larger boat."

"But do they have enough food and drink if they're delayed?"

"That could be their big problem," he acknowledged. "Unless they went too far away they could always make it back to the *Belle Corliss*."

"Barnabas would be there to greet them," she said in a

small voice.

"Still worrying about him?" Nathan said with some disdain.

"You forget I was in love with him once," she said.

"He was never worthy of you!"

"The Barnabas I first knew was. If he could somehow rid himself of that curse," she said.

"He never will," the young man warned her. "You should try and get some sleep before we face that burning sun again."

"I can't sleep," she said with a tiny shiver. "I'm frightened."

He reached for her. "Rest in my arms," he said gently. And as she settled in the protection of his encircling arms he touched his lips to hers and she responded. And eventually sleep came to her in the solace of this man she had come to love.

Morning came and with it the torture of the burning sun. The land which Nathan had predicted they might see with daylight had not come into view.

So Nathan still strained at the oars while she scanned the horizon hoping to see some sign of a passing vessel. She said, "How long can we exist this way?"

His pleasant face was heavy with weariness. "If we are careful of the remaining food and water we could go on for days if we're lucky."

"If we're lucky?" she repeated, not understanding.

He eyed her grimly. "There are even worse things than this blazing sun," he warned. "The weather can change and swiftly. If a blow comes up, a truly bad one, we could capsize in a matter of minutes."

"Oh, no!" she said in dismay at this new danger she hadn't thought of before.

"Don't panic," he said with a bitter smile. "The weather seems to be holding."

They suffered through the long day. Many times her throat was parched to the point of misery. But she would not ask for an extra ration of water since she knew the need might be greater later. Every so often Nathan took a respite from the oars only to tackle them again with renewed energy. She had begun to see it as a futile gesture and wished she dared tell him so. It seemed more practical that he conserve his energy and let the boat drift.

The provisions and other necessaries were stowed under a canvas covered area in the bow of the small boat. Nathan would reach under from time to time and bring out what they required. Clare spent most of her time in the stem of the tiny craft. And she fancied herself a grimy, bedraggled shadow of the pampered Lady Clare Duncan whose wit and beauty had graced Mayfair.

Dusk had begun to arrive. And it seemed to her the

overhead clouds were dark, although she did not mention this to Nathan. But she vividly recalled his prediction of what could happen in a sudden and violent storm. And she thought he was more subdued and grim than usual. Up until now he had done his best to bolster her spirits.

Once again he eased the oars and stared about him. The waves were just a trifle angrier, confirming her suspicions that the weather was going to worsen.

Then he rose to his feet and strained to study the horizon. After a moment he turned to her his face alive with joy. "Land! I can see it faintly! We've managed after all!"

She wanted to jump up and dance her joy. Her eyes filled with tears of thankfulness. Nathan was working at the oars with the energy of a madman. And within a short time she too was able to see the thin shadow of land on the horizon.

"Can we make it before dark?" she asked anxiously.

"We should," he managed as he gasped for breath from his exertions.

Miraculously, the land came quickly nearer. They actually did manage to bring the small boat in on a section of deserted beach as daylight was finally fading. Nathan helped her out of the boat onto the sand of the beach.

He glanced anxiously up at the rocky wilderness. "It's hard to say how far we are from any community."

"That doesn't matter," she said with a weary smile. "We're on land. We'll live!"

Nathan smiled at her in return. "I'd say that was likely," he agreed.

They were about to take the bag with her things in it and a jug of water and some food from the boat when a completely unexpected thing happened. They were only a few feet from the grounded boat when there was a stirring from under the canvas. They watched with disbelief as a giant bat fluttered from the dark place and went flying up into the night air high above their heads to vanish over the land.

Nathan was still staring after the weird creature. "I told you he could use his supernatural powers."

She gave him a startled look. "You think—?"

"Of course it was Barnabas," he told her. "This was his means of escape. Before the night is over he'll be looking for some pretty throat to revive himself."

Clare stood there still stunned. "I suppose I should regret that he has survived."

Nathan's face was compassionate. "But you don't, do you?"

"I'm afraid not," she admitted. "I think he deserves the

chance to free himself of the curse."

"If that's ever possible," Nathan said. "We'd better get those things and try scrambling up the hillside before it's completely dark. We haven't the benefit of wings like your friend Barnabas."

Before midnight they reached an isolated cabin where they were given shelter from the storm that had finally broken and the next day secured transportation to the nearest town. From there it was a short journey to the railway that eventually took them to New York City where Clare was able to draw money on her Boston account. They were married in New York in a small church near the waterfront and spent their honeymoon in a hotel on Fourteenth Street.

Once they'd recovered from the ordeal they'd been through she found Nathan Forbes restless and almost despondent. The fact he'd deserted the *Belle Corliss* hung heavy over him.

As he told her one day in the living room of their hotel suite, "I daren't let the authorities know I've survived. I'd be in disgrace. I'd never be given command of another ship."

"Then pretend you are dead," she told him. "We can go back to London. My father owns a major interest in several shipping firms. He can get you a command by simply saying the word."

He smiled at her wryly. "As easy as that?"

"As easy as that," she assured him. "We can sail the seven seas together for as long as you like."

His smile left him. "The *Belle Corliss* will always remain on my conscience."

"You deserted her for me," she said tenderly. "Is property more valuable than human lives?"

"I've gone the rounds of the shipping offices," he said. "And the *Belle Corliss* is listed as missing. Presumed lost."

"I suppose so. There was that awful storm that followed our reaching shore."

He nodded. "I doubt she survived that blow. Or any of the crew in the longboat either."

"It seems we should have had some word about them if they had managed to get to shore."

"A pretty tale they would have to tell of murders, vampires and violence," he said.

She got up and went close to him. "Then we can leave for London? My father will welcome you. I promise."

Nathan frowned. "Wait just a week or two longer. I'd like to be sure about the *Belle Corliss*. If there's no further word by then we'll take the first available steamer bookings to London."

Clare kissed him and he gave her a warm hug. She said, "I'll be glad when you've forgotten all about the *Belle Corliss*."

She didn't know then that this never would happen. That even when they were both old, with a host of grandchildren, the *Belle Corliss* would be prominent in their memories. But that was how it was to be.

The strange news came to them from the New York daily newspaper which Nathan purchased every morning. He came rushing into her bedroom and interrupted her as she finished with her hair before the dresser mirror.

"News at last!" he cried.

She turned to him with a startled look on her pretty face. "What sort of news?"

"They've found the *Belle Corliss*!"

"Really?"

He nodded with excitement and began to read from the newspaper account: "The *Belle Corliss* was located and boarded by a square-rigger out of Gloucester. They found her drifting on a calm ocean with no sign of crew or passengers on board. The boats were gone but everything else was in order, even to a porridge pot left on the stove. Nor were there any hints of violence or mutiny beyond some bloodstains found on the forward deck. It is likely the truth of what happened to the crew of the schooner will never be known, nor their reasons for leaving a seaworthy ship in such haste. The schooner is being claimed as salvage by the Gloucester shipping firm and it is probable this closes the books on the disappearance of the *Belle Corliss*. What happened aboard her is likely to always remain a mystery."

"And so it should," Clare exclaimed. "We're finally free. Can we go back to England now, my husband?"

He smiled as he took her in his arms to kiss her, "Yes, my lady."

At dusk a month later she was standing at the railing of the steamship Everglades as it was about to pull away from the New York wharf. Nathan had gone to talk to the purser about a piece of missing luggage so she found herself bidding America good-bye alone. The dock was thronged with people seeing the great ship on her way. And as it began to move from the wharf Clare thought she suddenly spied a familiar caped figure carrying a black cane. Then the man stepped close to the edge of the wharf and waved. And she was sure. Even from a distance in the fading light she could not mistake the gaunt, handsome face.

She waved frantically. "Barnabas, good-bye!"

He was smiling and he shouted back to her. And somehow his voice carried faintly above all the other voices and commotion. "Farewell, Lady Clare Duncan!"

"Lady Clare Duncan!" the stout vicar of Collinsport exclaimed. "How remarkable! The initials do fit, you know. Lady C.D."

Victoria turned to the visitor from England in surprise. "How could you possibly know, Mr. Collins?"

The smile on the gaunt, handsome face was sad. "I found that name among my grandfather's papers. When the vicar mentioned Lady C.D. just now it automatically came into my mind. I doubt if it could be the same person."

"But I believe it likely was," the vicar said enthusiastically. "We must go further into this. Perhaps you could send me some photostatic copies of the references to the lady. I'm most anxious to complete the history of Stormcliff."

"That would be a worthwhile project," Barnabas Collins agreed. "The town is fortunate to have someone as interested in its past as you undoubtedly are."

The vicar beamed. "I find the past fascinating, don't you, sir?"

"Indeed I do," Barnabas agreed with a slight twinkle in his eyes. "It has a special interest for me."

"Well, we mustn't lose ourselves in history and forget the good things of life. Would you and Miss Winters join me in some tea and cakes?"

"I'm really not hungry," Barnabas Collins said rising. "Some other time perhaps." He turned to smile at Victoria. "Unless Miss Winters would like some?"

Victoria was also on her feet. "I think not," she said. "We've talked quite a while. It's getting late. Elizabeth will start to worry about us."

The vicar smiled amiably. "Well, some other evening, then." And he saw them to the door. Just before Barnabas and Victoria stepped out into the darkness together the vicar said, "I imagine Collinsport has a special appeal for you, sir."

"Indeed it has," Barnabas said with one of his gracious smiles. "I find that I somehow keep coming back to it."

COMING SOON FROM
HERMES PRESS

...and over a dozen more thrilling *Dark Shadows* editions!

DARK SHADOWS

Published by **Hermes** Press

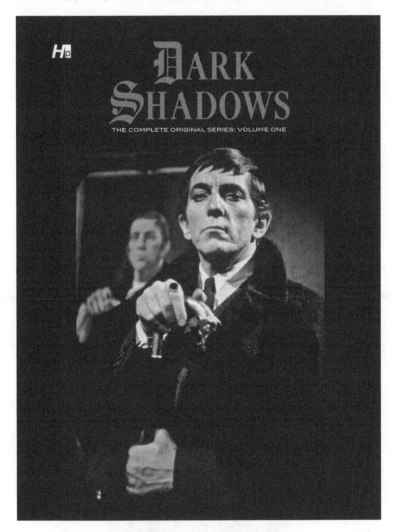

COMING SOON
Dark Shadows: The Complete Series: Volume 1
SECOND EDITION
From the Gold Key Comics 1968-1970
www.hermespress.com

DARK SHADOWS

Published by **Hermes** Press

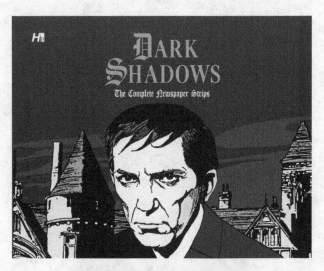

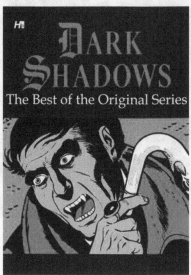